THE ONE DOLLAR
RIP-OFF

THE ONE DOLLAR
RIP-OFF

Ralph Dennis

ISBN: 1941298842
ISBN-13: 978-1-941298-84-8

Published by
Brash Books, LLC
12120 State Line #253,
Leawood, Kansas 66209
www.brash-books.com

PUBLISHER'S NOTE

This book was originally published in 1976 and reflects the cultural and sexual attitudes, language, and politics of the period.

CHAPTER ONE

H ump Evans and I were in George's Deli on North Highland. The front door and the back one were propped open. A cool pleasant breeze, the kind you expected in the spring, blew the length of the place. From our seats at the rear of the bar, I could look past Hump and see, out the back door, the gold and old leather colors of fall leaves.

It was Indian summer in Atlanta. Mid-October and the weather seemed stuck in deep tire ruts. The mornings were cool and the afternoons warm. The rapid changes had coughs and colds built in and I could hear the hack-hacks muffled by cupped hands here and there at the bar or in the booths.

It was a Monday. The day before, Marcy and I had done the Atlanta fall thing, the slow drive up to the mountains and back to see the leaves. I think I saw about half the people in Atlanta up there. It's an odd ritual anyway. You can see just as many leaves by driving around any Atlanta neighborhood.

Monday's a slow time in Atlanta. It's especially that way if you live the kind of life Hump and I do. We do just enough to get along and the shadow world business pays better and that's the kind of work we do. When there's work. A lot of afternoons we count the time in beer bottles and empty glasses. And once or twice a week we drop by George's for the corned beef. It's either a late lunch or an early supper. When you're not doing the nine to five, the regular hours, it doesn't much matter.

After a time the bartender, Sam Najjar, grows on you. He's a retired army warrant officer and there's a sneaky humor floating around just behind his eyeballs. You have to know him for a time before he'll throw a verbal curve at you. He's a fact man too and one whole shelf behind the bar is stacked with sports record and fact books. He'll talk football and basketball and hockey but his real sport is baseball. I don't think he's missed a Braves opening day or a Sunday game since he retired and moved back to town.

When Sam's not busy, he leans on the bar and sucks on a chunk of rank cigar and talks sports. He knows that Hump, black and six-seven and two-seventy or so, used to play defensive end at Cleveland and he respects Hump's opinion. This particular afternoon we were talking about the Monday night game. It matched the Bills and the Jets. O.J. was probably going to have another hell of a year and even if Joe Willie's knees squeaked his arm was still good.

We'd about worn out what we knew about both teams when the blond-haired bartender from Moe's and Joe's, the bar a few doors down from George's, leaned in at our end of the bar and handed Sam a sheet of paper.

Sam looked down at it. "What's this?"

"Hundred-dollar pool on tonight's game. Two spaces left."

Sam nodded and unclipped a pen from the half dozen or so he wore in his shirt pocket. He wrote SAM in one space and pushed the sheet away. I was reaching for my pocket when Hump slid the paper toward him. He used Sam's pen to write HUMP in the last space.

I mumbled at him and turned the pool sheet toward me.

Hump said, "Sorry, Jim. Maybe next time."

The pool sheet had ten lines down and ten lines across. That divided it into a hundred spaces and all of them were filled, usually by only a first name and a last initial.

Hump gave the bartender his dollar. "When'll you have the numbers?"

"We'll draw them now." The bartender from Moe's and Joe's folded Hump's dollar across a thick wad. "I'll bring the sheet back in a few minutes."

He left. Hump grinned at me. "Don't get your mad up. The odds are hell on a pool like this."

"And you're all kindness, saving me from losing my dollar?"

"That's it," Hump said. "Better me than you."

We had a couple of beers before the Moe's and Joe's guy returned with the pool sheet. He walked it down the bar. When he reached Hump, I leaned over Hump's shoulder and read the news with him. The down column was the Jets and Hump's number was a 3. The across column was the Bills and Hump's number there was a 3 also. That meant that the last number on each team's final score had to be a 3 for Hump to win: 33 to 13, 13 to 3, 23 to 13 ... anything like that. From the look Hump gave me, I knew that it was damned unlikely. For the 3's to show up, there'd have to be some missed extra points or some combinations of touchdowns and field goals.

After the bartender took the pool sheet away and Sam moved down the bar to open a couple of beers, Hump winked at me. "I'll sell you a half interest in my winner for a dollar."

I laughed at him.

"You're not going to believe this."

Hump stood in the doorway. It was late the next morning and I'd slept in. The coffee water had just started its boil when he rang the doorbell.

"You always say that." I waved him inside.

"This time..."

"What won't I believe?"

He followed me into the kitchen and hooked a toe behind a chair leg and pulled it out. "You watch the game last night?"

I shook my head. I'd watched the first half. Play had been listless and disinterested. Cosell gave me heartburn anyway, his pompous misuse of language, and neither Joe Willie nor O.J.

had done much for my attention span. I'd given up and gone to bed.

"Want to guess the final score?"

"Nothing to nothing on the basis of what I saw." I cut the burner and reached for another cup for Hump. He shook his head and got a glass from the cabinet. He sniffed the milk and poured himself a glass.

"Twenty-three to three," Hump said. "I hit the pool."

"Show me the money."

Hump poured back about half the glass of milk. "That's the part you're not going to believe."

He'd watched the game at his apartment. At first, he'd felt about the game the way I did. But the fact there wasn't any scoring in the first half didn't bother him. His chances for the hundred were still good. He wasn't out of it yet.

The Bills scored twice near the beginning of the third quarter. The second extra point blew wide to the right. 13. Hump thought that was a good stopping point for the Bills. He began to pull for the New York defense. Near the end of the third quarter the Jets got on the board with a field goal. 13 to 3. That was enough. That was the winner. Hump pulled for both defenses and against both offenses. No more points. *Stop.*

A Bills drive a couple of minutes into the final quarter bogged down at the thirty. The Bills kicker aimed it straight between the posts. 16 to 3. Hump mixed himself another drink and wrote the hundred off. Somebody else was going to spend it.

They played the next ten minutes or so of the game around the midfield mark. No score. No drives by either team. It was that way until about the three-minute mark. The Jets reached midfield. It was third down and six to go. Joe Willie dropped back to pass. His arm was back, not moving, when the Bills tackle hit him. The ball flipped end over end. A surprised linebacker scooped it up and ran almost forty yards for the touchdown. The score was 22 to 3. Hump leaned forward and watched the extra point try. The kick went through straight and good.

That made it 23 to 3 and it remained that way until the end of the game. At the final gun Hump switched off the TV set and stood up. Of course, he could wait until the next day. The hundred would be waiting. Still, he was wide awake. Not about to sleep for a few hours yet. Why not pick up the hundred and spend a bit of it bar-hopping? It was found money anyway.

Hump parked next to the fire station and walked the block to Moe's and Joe's. He passed George's Deli. Usually they closed early. Moe's and Joe's was packed from wall to wall. It was like that most nights. It was a hangout for Emory students, going back to the days when De Kalb County was dry. De Kalb was wet now but the tradition kept the students driving those extra miles into Fulton County.

Humped leaned on the front end of the bar until a bartender found him. "What'll you have?"

"I'm checking on the pool," Hump said. "I won it"

The bartender looked at Hump for a long moment. He shook his head and said, "Just a minute." He put his back to Hump and opened a file cabinet. He dug around in there until he found the pool sheet. He unfolded it and placed it on the bar. "Show me."

The light wasn't good. It took Hump a few seconds to find the 3's and pinpoint the space where they crossed. But he didn't find his name. He found where it had been written. Now it was blacked out by a pencil smear and another name had been written above it. JOHNNY B.

"I'm right under that smear," Hump said.

"Must have sold your space," the bartender said.

"No way," Hump said. "I'd like my hundred."

"He's already picked it up."

"Who?"

RALPH DENNIS

"That guy." The bartender turned the pool sheet toward him. "Johnny B."

Hump straightened up. He looked toward the back of the bar. It was dark and crowded and he couldn't see much. "Where's the blond guy put the pool together?"

"He's in the kitchen."

"I want to see him," Hump said.

"He's busy right now."

Hump leaned forward and placed his hands palm down on the bar. "Now you may not think a hundred is much money." He kept his voice level and easy, the threat out of it. "But when that hundred is mine by all rights I'll kick ass and knock heads. You get him from the kitchen."

The bartender started away. Hump dropped a dollar on the bar. "Give me a Bud first."

He was sipping the beer and staring out at the street when the blond bartender he'd seen at George's stopped at his elbow. He was wearing an apron now and there was the smell of hamburgers and grease and chili powder about him.

"You want to see me?"

"You remember me from this afternoon?"

They moved from the bar and stood next to the cigarette machine. The blond bartender nodded. "You took the last space."

"That's right. Get the pool sheet."

They held the sheet in the light from the front of the cigarette machine. "I had three and three," Hump said. He touched the space with a fingertip. "Somebody marked me out. That's my name under there."

The bartender turned the sheet. They could read HUMP in the deep impression on the back side of the paper. "You didn't sell it?"

"No."

The bartender read him and believed him. "That guy, Johnny, was drinking at George's. Let's see if he's still there."

It was a step away from closing time at George's. At one back table four or five student types labored over a final large pitcher. A couple of old-timers hunched at the bar. George and Sam looked bored and sleepy.

The Moe's and Joe's bartender stopped in front of Sam. "The man that won the pool ..."

"The one in the raincoat?"

"Him."

"He didn't stay long," Sam said. "He bought a round for the people he was drinking with and left."

"That was my winning number," Hump said.

Sam lifted an eyebrow. "Three and three?"

"Yeah."

"That's funny," Sam said. "I heard Joe Bottoms sell that guy his spot for a dollar. That guy said he wished he was in the pool and Joe offered him his numbers."

"Joe Bottoms wasn't in the pool," the blond bartender said. "I asked if he wanted in and he said he didn't."

"He sold a spot he didn't have?" Sam shook his head slowly.

"That's brass," Hump said.

"If you were going to sell somebody a spot you didn't have you'd pick unlikely numbers. A three and a three, for example. That's almost impossible. And if the numbers don't hit who's going to know that two people were waiting out that space? Who checks on a losing spot?"

"Why?" Hump asked.

The blond bartender shook his head.

"Why'd he do it?" Sam dipped a shoulder. "Joe's something of a wiseass. Even if he's got cash, he'd like to con a dollar off somebody. It's enough for two drafts and a phone call."

On the street outside George's, the bartender said he'd get in touch with Joe Bottoms and make him good for the hundred.

"I'll give you a day," Hump said.

"Look, we'll straighten it out. It's not worth ..."

"You got a hundred on you?"

"No." The bartender did a quick step toward Moe's and Joe's.

"If you had a hundred and I took it off you, would it bother you?"

"I guess so."

"That's my hundred," Hump said. "Don't talk reasonable shit to me."

The bartender waited. He didn't know what would happen next.

"And you run a fucked-up pool," Hump said.

"If we don't get the money off Joe Bottoms, we'll make the hundred good."

"You bet your ass you will." Hump turned and walked down Highland toward the fire station. At the corner, he looked back. The blond bartender stood there, staring down at the pool sheet in his hands.

"How did this guy, Bottoms, do it?" I asked.

Hump rinsed his glass and placed it in the sink. "He walks over to Moe's and Joe's. He asks for the sheet so he can get his numbers. It's probably one of the other bartenders. He's busy and he gives Bottoms the pool sheet and walks away. The rest is easy. He takes an unlikely combination of numbers and he marks out my name and writes in Johnny B. Then he goes back over and tells the guy his numbers are three and three."

"Heavy balls," I said.

"Or stupidity," Hump said.

"The odds were with him."

"For a dollar? All that crap for a dollar?"

"You put it like that," I said, "and I'd have to agree with you." I looked at him. In the years I'd known Hump, he came across as one of the more generous men I'd ever known. You needed a hundred and he had it and it was yours. Even if it left him short. Money didn't mean that much to him. This was, I saw, a whole different game. He'd been ripped off by a smartass and it burned him. It burned him right to the gut. But it wasn't the hundred. He'd have been as mad if it was a five-dollar bill.

"You got plans for the day, Hump?"

"Thought I'd wander about town a bit. Might get to Moe's and Joe's at six o'clock."

"And then?"

"They don't have my hundred and I might see if I can find Joe Bottoms."

I grinned at him. "Need company?"

He grinned back. "Not help," he said. "Just company."

CHAPTER TWO

Aimless afternoon in downtown Atlanta. A drink here and a drink there. A light buzz warming us, we sat in the outdoor courtyard of Peachtree Center and watched the lunchtime girls stride by. From the way they dressed, you'd think it was spring. dressed

At four-thirty, we got Hump's Buick from the Davison's parking deck and pointed it toward North Highland. It was bad timing. We bogged down in the late-afternoon, after-work traffic.

It was a bit after five when Hump parked the Buick across the street from Moe's and Joe's. A few doors back from that bar I could see the open door at George's Deli.

"It's too early," Hump said.

"A couple at George's?"

"Why not?" Hump stepped out and stood in the street, staring at the front of Moe's and Joe's. Nothing came of it. Nobody ran out with a fistful of bills and offered them to him.

Sam had the two Buds open and on the bar by the time we cleared the deli and Middle Eastern grocery part of the place. Hump dropped a five on the counter. Sam picked it up and gave it a mock-serious stare. "This part of the hundred, Hump?"

Hump laughed with him. "Not yet."

Sam laughed all the way to the cash register and back. "Those boys will have a hard time putting together another pool."

"That's what they get for running it like a Chinese fire drill," I said.

"They're trying." Sam counted out Hump's change. "Since I came to work at three, they've been over two or three times trying to find out how they can reach Joe Bottoms."

Hump drank from the bottle. "They learn much?"

"Nothing worth much." Sam looked down the bar. Nobody needed a refill. "A house painter comes in here said he thought Joe used to drive one of those catering trucks, the ones that go from area to area selling sandwiches and soft drinks."

"Used to?"

"He thinks Joe quit that job a month or two back."

Hump shook out one of my smokes and lit it. "That's a lot of help."

"Someone else... I forget who it was... said he thought Joe did part of his drinking at the Parkland. That's the place..."

"I know it," Hump said.

I leaned in. "No word where he lives?"

"Nothing recent and he's not listed in the phone book."

"That means they don't have my hundred yet," Hump said.

"That's my guess."

Hump thanked Sam and we carried our beers to the round table next to the jukebox. I fed a couple of quarters to the machine and punched some Merle Haggard and Willie Nelson. At six, we left George's and walked down the street to Moe's and Joe's.

No help. As we'd figured. The blond bartender said he hadn't been able to reach Joe Bottoms yet. He was nervous and shaky when he talked and he wouldn't look Hump in the eyes. But, he said, he would keep on trying no matter how long it took. If it took a week.

He had the manners to offer us a beer on the house but Hump shook that off. Hump wasn't in the mood for any of that friendly crap.

Before we left Moe's and Joe's, Hump got a fairly good description of Joe Bottoms. Five-ten or eleven. Straw blond hair worn long. About a hundred and eighty pounds. Stoop-shouldered.

Sleepy, hooded eyes. Usually he wore tennis shirts, jeans and a red University of Georgia nylon warm-up jacket.

A few minutes later, we parked next to the Highland branch of the library and jaywalked over to the Parkland.

It was wino country. Hard luck country. The last chance to make good had left on a Greyhound bus a month ago. The loving woman who used to open the cans and warm the soup had gone home to her mother in Macon. That kind of place. Just the beer and the wine left. Get it and drink it and let the rest of the world sweat that dry thirst.

"Deliver me," Hump said when he brought two drafts to the booth I'd staked out.

I knew what he meant. I felt the same way. It wasn't a pleasant thought. That chance that, in a few years, we might be the ones waking in the morning with the dry, scratchy throats. The rest of the day would stretch out, measuring a hundred years, when we'd have to worry about getting enough wine to make it through the night. The begging and the lying and all the sweat time that went with it.

"Save your money," I said.

"I've got another idea. We start putting in wine now. Bottles and bottles, cases and cases. We fill a couple of rooms with it. And then, when we're old and we turn wino, we'll have a lifetime supply."

"Or save your money," I said, "and buy a wine store and just move a bed in."

The booth I'd taken was off to the right, partly blocked from the sight line to the front door by the corner of the bar. Most of what the bar sold was the tap beer. There wasn't a waiter or a waitress and we watched the traffic to the bar and back. That was good for a few minutes. Dull after that. So, I turned in the booth and watched the back door. Now and then one or two of the winos would hitch up their trousers and pat their hip pockets and head for the john. I knew what that meant. I'd been in the john once when a wino had walked in. He'd uncapped a pint of white port and poured it all down without taking the bottle from his mouth. It had to be done that way because the Parkland didn't have a license to sell wine for drinking on the premises. It was all take-out and the quickie in the john was the way around that. Still, the management had to know. It was hard to ignore the huge metal trash can half full of wine bottles.

Seven o'clock. I was hungry. A trip to the deli counter and a look at the meats and I settled for a bag of peanuts.

Eight o'clock. I was bloated. The bloat without a belch in it. I wasn't high, nothing like that. I sat and looked at a full glass of draft and didn't want to touch it.

Nine. I eased out of the booth and shook my head at Hump. "I've had it."

"Where to?"

"I need about a pound of prime rib."

He pushed his glass away and stood up. "Something to eat and I can drop by and look in on the way home."

"That's it."

I stopped just outside the front door. From the inside there hadn't been any way to know. It was raining now. Maybe it had just started. I hadn't noticed anyone entering the Parkland with the rain marks on him. We stood under the awning and looked at the rain. It was steady and solid and it didn't look as if it would go away for a long time.

"No reason for both of us to get wet," Hump said. "I'll get the car and ..."

I touched his arm and stopped him. I'd been looking in the direction of Ponce de Leon. I'd seen a man round the corner at St. Charles. He was moving slow, not paying much attention to the rain. When he passed under a streetlamp, I saw that he was wearing a red nylon warm-up jacket. He looked about the right size too.

"Might be your man," I said.

"Let's see." We stepped out into the rain and headed for him. At nine the block was empty. The drugstores had closed earlier and only the night lights burned in the Highland library.

We met the man in the red jacket five doors away from the Parkland. We'd taken the street side of the walk, forcing him to settle for the building side. When we were level with him Hump turned his head toward the man and said, "That you, Joe?"

The man stopped. He said, "Yeah. Who are...?"

Hump moved fast. He rammed a shoulder into Joe Bottoms and slammed him against a brick storefront. I heard the breath jet out of him. I circled him and caught his right arm at the elbow and pinned it where it was.

"The name's Hump."

I could see his face. His eyes weren't sleepy and hooded now. "I don't know anybody named..."

"It's a matter of a hundred dollars," Hump said.

"The pool?"

"Now you've got it," Hump said.

I looked in both directions. No movement. We were almost level with Hump's Buick.

"I don't have it on me," Joe Bottoms said, "but I can get it."

I didn't like doing our business on the street. It wasn't a high-crime area but the Atlanta police did patrol it now and then. I didn't want to be taken for a mugger. I said, "Let's talk in the car."

"That all right with you, Joe?"

"I... I..."

"Keys?" I put out a hand and Hump slapped the key ring into it. "Got him?"

Hump grunted yes. I released the elbow and stepped away. A few fast steps and I reached the Buick. I unlocked the door and held it open. Hump, one hand on Joe Bottoms' wrist and the other pinching his shoulder, brought him across the street and pushed him head first into the back seat. Hump lunged in after him. I got behind the wheel. After the engine kicked over, I drove toward Highland and Virginia.

Behind me, Hump said, "A hundred dollars is not much to kill a man over."

Joe Bottoms mumbled something.

"Speak up, Joe."

"I said I'd make it good."

"You hurt my pride," Hump said. "You know how silly this makes me look?"

"And dumb too," I said.

"Shut up." Hump sounded angry at me. "You're trying to get me mad so I'll kick the shit out of this pretty boy. You want to watch."

"It don't matter to me one way or the other," I said.

"Then shut up about it."

It was a game we were doing. A simple whipsaw.

I said, "You don't have to talk to me like that. I'm not the one made you look dumb."

At Virginia, I took a left and headed away from the lights. From Virginia to Monroe it was a residential district. That meant there weren't a lot of lights to worry about.

"Quit talking about dumb," Hump said. "The next thing anybody knows I'm going to be spending that hundred. Who's going to laugh at me then?"

"If you get the hundred," I said.

"How much money you got on you, Joe?" Hump had shifted gears. He was soft and reasonable.

"Nine or ten dollars."

"That's not even a down payment," Hump said. "That won't even buy my supper."

I stopped at a red light. I looked over the seat back at them. You could smell the scared sweat. "Maybe Joe's got something he could pawn with us."

"What do you mean … us? It's my hundred we're talking about."

The light changed. I went back to driving. "I don't want any part of that hundred. It's bad luck money."

"Bad luck only if I don't get it," Hump said.

"Make up your mind," I said. We were passing the old Marta bus barn. "I don't intend to drive around all night."

"Where you live, Joe?"

"Maybe he's got a piggy bank or a coin collection."

"I'll take pennies if you've got enough of them," Hump said.

I eased to the curb. Right ahead Virginia dead ended at Grady High School. "Tell the man where you live."

"Look, give me a day or two. I'll meet you somewhere and I'll have the hundred for you."

"No sale on that trash," Hump said. "You've got a way of dropping out of sight. I've got better things to do with my time than look for you."

I gave the seat back a hard slap. "Hump, dammit, which way you want me to go?"

"Joe, I am not going to like it if you bleed on my upholstery."

"I'm not going to bleed …" Joe broke it off. He understood.

"Which way?" I slammed the seat back again.

"Joe?"

"Left," Joe said, "take a left."

That part was done. We'd sold him that hard-assed bill of goods.

It was a one-story duplex on St. Charles. It was a wide loop drive and a circle to get there. It was, as I parked and looked toward Highland, only a short walk to the Parkland where we'd started out.

Both sides of the duplex were dark. The driveway was empty. Joe sandwiched between us, we hiked up the walk past the neat lawn. Maybe the landlord cared. Joe didn't look the type who'd rake a leaf or walk behind a lawn mower.

Joe Bottoms used his key to unlock the door. I pushed him toward Hump and went in first. I found the switch to the overhead light and flipped it on. Behind me, Hump gave Joe a shove and sent him stumbling past me.

It was a dollhouse of an apartment. The room we'd entered was supposed to look like a living room but the Castro couch was still extended to form a bed. The sheets were twisted and the pillowcase looked brown and dirty, as though it hadn't been changed in a couple of months. Straight ahead, past the sofa bed, was a partition with an opening and a counter. I could see, through the opening, that this was the kitchen with a two-burner gas stove and a battered old refrigerator. There was a high stool with a back to it at the counter and the paper plate on the counter told me that he used that area as a dining room. I opened the closed door off to the left. It was the bathroom. That was it.

Hump stared down at the bed. "Our friend here is not very neat."

"He wasn't expecting company." I pulled the bathroom door closed and leaned into the kitchen for a closer look.

"See anything worth pawning?"

"Not in here." I joined them in the living room-bedroom. It looked like most of what was in the apartment came with the lease. The tiny portable black and white TV set was probably his but you couldn't get ten dollars for it at one of the shops on Pryor. "Nothing," I said.

"Boy, you're in trouble," Hump said.

"I can have the hundred tomorrow," Bottoms said. He looked pale and shaky in the strong overhead light. I had the feeling he was about to break down and cry.

"Tonight's the right time," Hump said. "Tomorrow it's overdue."

"I swear I can have it."

"I don't believe you. That's my last word. Anybody who has to trick a dollar off some dumb ass ..."

"That was fun," Bottoms said. "I was playing."

I gave the apartment a last slow look. It was pressure and game time again. "I don't want to watch this. I'll wait in the car, Hump." I got to the door and twisted the knob before it broke him down to the split.

"Wait. I can prove it."

I put my back to the door and watched Bottoms lunge for the clothes closet. "Hump, watch him ..."

Hump had the same idea. There might be iron in the closet somewhere. Hump reached the closet just behind Bottoms. Hump put one hand on his shoulder and leaned in with him. Bottoms felt around on the top shelf off to the right. His hand grabbed something. It wasn't iron or a weapon of any kind. It was a plain white envelope. Hump swung about with him. Bottoms put his back to us. He dug into the envelope. When he turned, he had a narrow piece of paper in one hand. Even as he held the piece of paper out to us, he stuffed the envelope into his hip pocket.

Hump held out his hand. Bottoms passed the paper to him. I moved over and looked at it with Hump. It was a check. The amount, $2,000, had been imprinted on it by a computer. It was drawn on the account of the Frank R. Temple Construction Company in Boston. The authorizing signature at the bottom right of the check had been applied by a check-writing machine.

"All I've got to do is cash that tomorrow," Bottoms said.

"Looks real," Hump said to me.

"Might be." The payee, Joseph Bottoms, was typed in.

"You see? Didn't I tell you the truth?" Joe Bottoms took a couple of steps toward Hump and reached for the check. "I cash this check tomorrow and you'll get your hundred."

Hump pushed his hand away. He folded the check and slipped it into his right-hand money pocket. "I've got a better use for it, Joe."

"Huh?"

"It's your guarantee," Hump said. "I'll be at George's tomorrow at five P.M. You have the hundred for me and you'll get your check back."

"No, look." The composure was gone. He was sweating. "I've got to have that check. I'm in trouble without…"

"No chance," Hump said.

"I got to have it."

"Tomorrow at five." Hump turned for the door.

It was desperation. That's all it could be. Joe Bottoms took a run and jumped on Hump's back, wrapping his arms around Hump's neck. Hump mumbled, "Shit, man," and broke Bottoms' grip with one hand. He whirled and threw Bottoms into the center of the sofa bed.

Bottoms curled up, the fight gone out of him, eyes closed as he reached for the pillow and dragged it toward him.

A short drive and we were at Colony Square. We had the prime rib at The Brothers Two. I had to pay the tab.

CHAPTER THREE

At five-thirty, Hump turned slowly on the bar stool and let his feet hit the floor. Without looking at me, he walked out of the bar section and into the deli section. He had to thread his way through a couple of Arab or Greek families who'd come all the way across town to buy the feta and the peta bread and the black olives in brine that came in the big orange plastic barrels.

At the front door, he stopped and looked back at me. He waved a *one* at me. I nodded and the next time Sam passed I ordered two more Buds. It was closer to five minutes before he returned. He shook his head and took the bar stool on my right. I pushed his fresh beer at him.

"Thought he might have misunderstood."

"He's not at Moe's and Joe's?"

He didn't bother to answer me. It was a dumb question anyway. "We'll give him until six."

"I thought he got the word."

"It looked that way to me," Hump said.

"That found hundred is turning into a lot of work. I'm glad I'm just along as company."

He gave me a bleak grin. "You've got to finish what you start."

I understood that. You finished even if it turned dumb and stupid on you.

"One thing. I've still got his check."

The check was bait and it hadn't worked. I didn't understand it. It was a hundred dollars against two thousand. A good exchange. No, staying away didn't make sense.

At six, I pushed the empties toward the back of the bar counter, nodded at Sam and got his wave as we left.

I waited in the car. I watched Hump, on the duplex porch, try Bottoms' door and then lean on the buzzer. Hump was a black mean shadow up there. Frustration was getting to him and I knew I'd have to do some song and dance to help him keep his balance. It was fair enough. He'd done the same thing for me a time or two.

It was bare light out. As far as I could see down St. Charles the leaves were turning. The first ones had already fallen and it would be December before the trees were bare. By the time you raked one dumping another one replaced it. That was why my rake was rusting and getting dusty in the garage. I'd wait until December and then hope that a big wind would come up and blow them into somebody else's yard.

Hump moved his hand away from the buzzer. He gave the door an angry shot or two with his palm. Nothing. Zero. He looked at me and blew his breath out slowly. He came down the steps and cut across the lawn.

I waited until he was behind the wheel. "You want to wait some more at the deli?"

He considered it. He chewed it for half a minute or so. In the end he shook his head. "I've got the check. It's up to him to find me."

He drove out Highland and parked in a space in front of George's. My car was down the street and around the corner next to the fire station.

I pushed the door open and hesitated. I hadn't done my song and dance yet. "Supper?"

"Brothers Two again?"

"Sure."

"Go on over and save me a spot at the bar." He tilted his head toward George's. "I want to leave a number with Sam in case Bottoms drops by later."

I had a couple of sips of the J&B and rocks at the bar. Down two booths a pair of advertising types were bullshitting each other in loud voices. All that pompous talk about creativity when all they were selling was toilet paper.

I felt blue and alone. Maybe part of that was the gray fall day. Womb days. I left my drink and smokes at the bar and found the pay phones. Marcy answered on the first ring. She wouldn't ever admit it, but I think she expected the call. No, she hadn't eaten yet. She said she'd meet us in thirty minutes. If she was really hungry, she might make it in forty-five and even that would be a record.

Hump and I were on our third drinks when she arrived. Part of the wait I spent kidding around with Truckee, the waitress we usually asked for. She'd caught my interest early, the first time I'd eaten at The Brothers Two. I'd looked up from the menu and I'd said, "What's good to eat?"

She'd looked at me with an impish half-grin and said, "Me."

Truckee's section was busy tonight. One more drink at the bar with Marcy and we had to settle for another waitress' section of tables. Hump stayed with the prime rib and Marcy went along with him. I changed over to the trout.

A good dinner in him and some aimless talk from Marcy and Hump appeared to have calmed down. We were doing the coffee when the paging system called his name. I lifted an eyebrow at him. Sliding out of the booth, passing me, he said, "I left this number too."

The time he was gone I gave Marcy a brief account of the one-dollar rip-off. When he returned, she watched him with a certain kind amusement.

"That Bottoms?"

He shook his head. "Somebody calling for him."

"Why?"

"He said Bottoms was a friend. Said Bottoms was out running around trying to get the last twenty or so of that hundred."

"Odd," I said.

"Tell me something new."

"Wait one." I grinned at Marcy and left the booth. At one of the pay phones I dialed George's Deli. Sam answered. "Did Bottoms come in after we left?"

"There was a call," Sam said.

"Was it Bottoms?"

"He said it was but it didn't sound like him. I wasn't sure what to do but I gave him the numbers Hump left with me. Is that all right?"

I told him that was fine and thanked him and hung up.

"Odd thing number two," I told Hump about the call to George's.

"That's also odd thing number three," Hump said. "I don't think that dude has this many friends."

"The call you got," I said.

"They want a meet with me. That is, Joe Bottoms is supposed to meet me at the Fifteenth Street side of the High Museum. In the driveway there."

"When?"

"They said half an hour. I said an hour."

I checked my watch. I estimated when the call had come in. That would put the meeting at nine-thirty, give or take a minute or two. "They give any reason why Bottoms doesn't just walk right in here and put the money in your hand?"

"I asked."

"And...?"

"They said he'd laid some bad paper on The Brothers Two a while back."

"They seem to have all the answers figured to all the possible questions."

"Don't they?"

I wagged my empty cup at our waitress and she brought the coffee pot. While she refilled my cup I said, "You will take my personal check, won't you?"

She laughed as though I was joking and then she ticked off the credit cards they accepted. After she moved away, I said: "That's it, unless they've changed the policy in the last year."

"Truckee'll take your check," Marcy said. I'd made the mistake of telling Marcy about my first meeting with Truckee. Now she didn't miss a chance to dig at me.

I shook my head. "She'd laugh louder."

The waitress brought the check. She remembered my question and dropped the check on Hump. Hump passed it across the table to me. "Tomorrow's my day."

"It better be." But I didn't mind. It had been a medium to poor summer. The dirty little jobs had been half-assed and the money didn't keep us in drinks. I was still living off my shoe box, the stash I fell back on in the hard times.

I counted out the cash to cover the face of the tab. I had some trouble with the tip. I hadn't liked that laugh. Ten per cent and to hell with it. I put the tray on the outside edge of the table and checked my watch. Half an hour had passed since Hump had received the call. "You leaving now?"

"I expect to be early," he said.

"You want me along?"

"It was just supposed to be company," he said.

"It's dark out there."

He cut his eyes toward Marcy. "Only if you've got the time."

I said I did. Marcy could drive to my place and wait for us. She had a key and she could let herself in. And, if we got the hundred, maybe Hump could spring for a bottle of Asti Spumante. It was a wine Marcy'd liked since the summer. I didn't. It was too sweet for me. I liked a trickle of brandy mixed in mine to fight the sugar.

"Deal," Hump said.

I watched Marcy's taillights vanish in the direction of the Strip and Tenth Street. I turned onto Fifteenth and parked there. Off to my right, past a lawn, was the spotlighted outline of the High Museum. After a minute or two, I got out of the car and crossed the street to the sidewalk. I could see the single car, Hump's Buick, parked in the loading and unloading zone. In the dim light, I could see the huge shape of Hump. He was outside his car, leaning on the roof of it.

I ignored him and walked toward the narrow street that ran behind the museum. I turned onto that street and curled back and crossed the back parking lot, headed back toward Hump. I stopped in the darkness, at the edge of the light, about fifty yards away from him. Ten minutes passed while Hump smoked a slow cigarette, the coal bobbing above the Buick's top. Another ten minutes went by the board while I fought the urge to have a smoke myself.

Nine-thirty. Time for the meet. Minutes dragged by. Hump had his back to me now, watching the Peachtree entrance to the loading and unloading zone.

After twenty minutes, at ten of ten, I knew it wasn't going to happen. It had been scrubbed for some reason. I gave a low sharp whistle. Hump turned and waved an arm at me. I followed the wave out of the dark and into the dim light thrown off by the floodlighted columns of the museum.

He met me partway. "I don't understand this shit."

I said I didn't either. They'd insisted on the meeting in half an hour and had settled for the one in an hour. They'd been eager but they'd backed away.

"Thanks anyway for backing me."

I said that the fresh air was probably good for me.

"I'm headed home," he said.

"Come by and have a drink with us."

"No way." He put a lazy, sneaky grin on me. "You young lovers need some time alone."

"I'll tell Marcy you said that."

"Marcy knows where my head is." He swung back to the Buick. I cut across the grass and reached Fifteenth where my Ford was parked. I was halfway across the street when a nervous thought hit me gut-low. I didn't like it. I turned in the middle of the street and waved an arm at him. Too late. Too late. He was pulling out of the High Museum lot, swinging right and heading for the Strip. I dropped the arm and ran for my car. I hit the horn a couple of times. That should have stopped him but it didn't. He honked back at me and kept going. By the time I got turned around and took a right onto Peachtree I couldn't see the Buick. He'd probably caught the green light on Fourteenth. I caught the red and had to wait it out.

He'd said he was headed home. Maybe. Maybe not. The mood he was in he might have changed his mind. There were a lot of bars in Atlanta and he knew the back way in at about a quarter of them.

His apartment was on the third floor. It overlooked the street. Second one over from the left front corner. I slowed down and looked up. No lights showing. That could mean something or not a damned thing.

All right, I might feel dumb. That was the risk. If his Buick wasn't in the side or the back parking lot it would be a year before I'd admit that I'd tracked him home on some wild-assed hunch. Or it might be two or three years. Or never.

After I passed the front of the apartment building, I took a left into the side parking lot. It was dark and that raked at me some. Other times there had been some kind of light. Not now. My headlights, as I slowed, lighted the spaces to my right. No sign of Hump's Buick. And I remembered that the illumination had come from a bulb over the side entrance to the building. Dark now.

The driveway doglegged left. There were more parking spaces in back. As soon as I turned the corner of the building my head-lights lit up the human charade.

Hump was in the center of it. He was backed up against his Buick, hands behind his head, legs spread. A stocky white man in a tan raincoat and a checkered hat stood about five paces away. He had Hump under the gun. A second man, black and slat lean, leaned close to Hump. He was searching Hump.

When my headlights struck them full both the men with Hump looked into the full beam. It was all the break Hump needed. He dropped his right hand and hit the black. The fist hit the man throat-high and drove him back into the white. The white pushed out and tried to clear the black. He wasn't fast enough. Hump closed with him, belly to belly, and grabbed the gun hand.

I braked and got out of the car. I swung a wide circle. I wanted to move in but I didn't like the way the gun was pointed. It was good sense. A round ripped into the asphalt in front of my Ford. I made the loop wider. I was about level with them, past the arc of the gun, when the black man scrambled to his feet. I could hear him gagging for air. He ran straight for me. I'd been watching the gun and I didn't have time to brace myself.

Maybe he didn't see me. Maybe it was panic. He hit me heart-high with the crown of his head. The force of that threw me ass-over in the air. When I landed my head hit the asphalt. I wasn't out and I put out my right arm and caught his leg. He jerked that leg away and tried to jump me. He didn't make it. He tripped but one foot hit my left hip and numbed that leg all the way down to the ankle. I expected him to follow up. Instead he got to his feet again and I could hear fast and light footsteps going away from me. My left leg didn't want to work. I forced it and crabbed around until I faced Hump.

The white was stronger than most. He'd put up a good struggle. Part of that might have been because Hump had to be careful with the gun. Now strength made the difference. Hump pulled the white around until he was next to the trunk of the Buick. He rammed the white's gun hand against the Buick until the man cursed and the gun fell free. Hump kicked it and it skidded toward me. It stopped two or three feet from me. The white man jerked away from Hump and ran for the gun. I crawled in that direction. I gave a last lunge and fell on top of the gun. I felt the hard metal scrape a couple of ribs.

At the last minute the white gave it up and skirted me.

I rolled away. One hand caught the gun butt. I turned and swung it toward the white but he'd turned the corner of the building.

Hump leaned over me. "You all right?"

"Go after him." I passed the gun to him.

Too late. We heard the engine race and somebody tore rubber. That was probably the black. He'd gone for the car, parked in the side lot, and started it and backed it out. He'd been ready when the white got there.

Hump caught me under the arms and pulled me to my feet. The hip could take the weight after all. I hadn't been sure it would. "It broke, Jim?"

"I don't think so."

I leaned against the Buick while he parked my Ford in a space down the row. When he returned my keys, I limped into the apartment building after him. At the elevator I said, "What were they after?"

"As if you hadn't guessed."

"The check."

He nodded. "That's what they said."

"Why?"

"I don't know."

"They get it?"

The elevator doors opened and we got on. Hump punched 3 and leaned a shoulder against the wall. He watched with some concern while I counted my ribs. I seemed to have an extra one or two.

"Another minute or two," Hump said, "and they might have found it." He lifted his right leg and pulled the pant leg up. He patted the elastic part of his knee-length socks. "If they got this far."

In Hump's apartment, I gave the white man's gun a look and dropped it on the sofa. It was a .38 Chief's model and it was so battered and scratched that any trace backward wouldn't lead anywhere. There'd probably been five or six owners and two or three pawnshops involved since it came out of the factory.

"For your collection," I said.

"Don't you want it?"

"I've got the Xerox on my ribs."

He mixed me a drink while I dialed my number. I told Marcy I'd be a little late. I said I'd be there as soon as I had hip surgery. Marcy didn't think it was funny.

As an afterthought, on the way out, I took the .38 Chief's with me. I polished it with my handkerchief and gave it a toss so that it landed on one of the putting greens when I drove through Piedmont Park on my way home.

Lord only knows the past on an old gun like that. I didn't want it around in case it carried ghosts with it.

CHAPTER FOUR

M y head didn't seem to want to work.

It might have been the drinks I had with Marcy after I drove home from Hump's apartment. She'd wanted to hear the story and I'd limped around, gritting my teeth, and told her my version. I made the crawl and leap for the gun sound like a scene from one of the World War II movies. You know the one. The cowardly kid from the slums jumps on the grenade and saves the lives of his buddies.

Marcy didn't believe it for a minute. She'd seen the same movies. So, I'd had to pull up my T-shirt and show her the scrape and blotch on my ribs. "See? See?"

She stayed the night.

I think I remember her kissing me before she left. On a scale from AWFUL to ALL RIGHT her morning mouth wasn't as bad as most. And there'd been the warm good smell of her in the sheets when I rolled over and went back to sleep.

The phone rang and my head didn't want to work. I rolled over and put my feet on the floor. I stood up and my left hip seemed to explode on me. I sat down slowly and felt the pain jumping and leaping from my knee to my shoulder. It was the fifth or sixth ring before I lifted the receiver and grunted into it.

"You all right, Jim?" It was Hump.

"I hope so." I told him that I'd decided to give up ballet now that I'd injured my hip. "What's with you?" I looked at my watch on the night table. It was nine thirty-four.

"This is my one phone call."

"Huh?" Head still not working. "What?"

"I'm at the De Kalb County police station."

"Why?"

"That Joe Bottoms. He turned up dead out here. Beat all to hell and shot. He had my name and phone number in his pocket."

"That all they got?"

"I don't think so." A pause. "They know about the rip-off and they know I was looking for him. They dropped by early this morning. One look at the scratches on my hands, the ones from the scuffle last night, and they decided I did the killing."

"All right," I said. I got up slowly and put some weight on the hip. "I'll be there with a lawyer or a character reference of some kind... or both. Give me an hour."

"These people aren't friendly. And there's so much water on the floor I have to swim to the johnny and back."

I told him to rest and broke the connection. First, I called the law office of a guy I'd met a couple of months back. He was Duke law school and all that and he liked his drinking and chasing and I'd met him at Harrison's a time or two. There wasn't any answer at his office. I tried his home number. I'd about decided he was between home and his office when he answered.

"James Fitch."

I told him who I was.

"Sure, I remember you," he said.

"Remember Hump Evans, the big dude I was with?"

He said he did.

"They've got him at De Kalb jail on a murder charge. No, that's not right. I'm not sure they've charged him yet."

"He do it?"

"I don't know when the killing took place. I was with him most of the afternoon and evening. If it happened during that time, he'd have had to do it while my back was turned."

"Your word good at De Kalb?"

"Probably not," I said. "You meet me there?"

"Give me an hour and a half. You see, you called while I was consulting with a young lady."

I laughed. That was like him.

The second call was to Art Maloney. His wife, Edna, answered. "He in bed yet?"

"A step away," Edna said. I heard her call him. While she waited, she asked about Marcy.

"She's fine," I said. "I took her to dinner last night."

"When are you going to drop by and see us? The boys ask about you all the time."

"Soon," I said and then Art was on the line.

At the end of my rundown he said he wasn't sure how much good he could do. But he'd go over with me if there was a chance he could help Hump. It would be unofficial and it might get his tail in a crack. I said I knew that Hump would appreciate it and that I'd pick him up in forty-five minutes.

After a shave and a shower, I got down my shoe box and got out five hundred. I didn't know what the bail might be or if he'd be allowed bail. Still, I thought I'd take the cash in case he needed a bondsman. Fitch, the lawyer, would know more about that.

Art and I arrived first. It's a big ugly building and the jail is on the basement level. It's a big lobby with displays of shoulder patches from police departments all over the country in glassed-in cases and there are a couple of hard benches and a wall phone and a listing of bondsmen. There's a notice next to the listing that says that the police don't recommend any of the bondsmen. No, that's not the way it sounds. There have been some scandals around the state where there were some connections between the police and bondsmen. One sheriff even owned a big part of one of the bonding companies.

There's a glassed-in window at the back of the lobby. I left Art and went over and leaned on the counter for a time before anybody noticed me. They were having a morning coffee break and laughing it up like cowboys and I watched the banks of closed-circuit monitors. It was mostly cellblock hallways and a parking lot or two. After five minutes, I went into a coughing fit and a fat cop with a doughnut in one hand and a cup of coffee in the other came over and grunted at me.

"Hump Evans," I said.

"The nigger?"

"Black," I said.

"You his lawyer?"

"A friend," I said. "The lawyer's on the way."

The fat cop went into an office off to the right. He rooted about on the desk in a pile of papers. He didn't find anything. Then he made a call. It was a short call, just a few words. When he returned, he choked down the last third of his doughnut before he said, "He's not charged yet. They're still interrogating him."

I looked over my shoulder at Art. I made room for him. Art showed his I.D. The fat cop looked at it and said, "Is this Fulton County business too?"

Art didn't answer that "Who's handling it?"

"Bowser's talking to the … black."

"Tell Bob that Art Maloney wants to see him."

"He know you?"

"He knows me," Art said.

While the cop made the call, Art and I sat down on one of the benches and had part of a smoke. The fat cop returned to the window a minute later and yelled that Bowser was on the way out.

Bowser's office smelled of stale smoke and socks that needed changing and an armpit or two. Bowser was in his mid-forties but he looked younger and he carried himself as though he'd been a Marine drill instructor or thought he should have been. His hair was in a brush cut, tipped with gray, and his eyes were red-rimmed and tired. While I sat down and looked at him, he put his back to us and fiddled with the blinds. After he swung around and faced us, I could see that he'd dismissed me as not mattering. His attention was on Art.

"Next week, Art," he said, "I'm going to drop by Decatur Street and mix in your business some."

"We'd be glad to have you," Art said. He kept it low and even. "Especially if you coming by kept us from making a mistake."

"What mistake? We haven't charged him yet."

"You going to?"

"We're still talking," Bowser said, "and he's not giving many answers."

"No answers at all?"

"All he'll say is that he was with a James Hardman most of the afternoon and evening." Bowser's eyes pecked at me and slid away.

"You got a time for the killing?"

"Right about at 8 P.M. last night."

"That exact?" I said.

"Within a minute or two," Bowser said. "A man who lives next to the wooded area where Bottoms was found says he was in the bathroom on the side of the house next to the woods. He says he heard what sounded like a scream and a muffled shot. He didn't think much of it at the time. He just went back in and watched his favorite program, one that comes on at eight."

"Evans was with me at eight," I said.

Bowser shook his head. "You're too tight with him. And I know about you and your word stinks."

I turned to Art. "Marcy was with us."

"That's two," Art said.

I worked it back through my mind. The call for Hump came in at about eight-thirty and we'd been there about an hour before that. "There are a lot more. From seven-thirty to nine we were in

The Brothers Two. There ought to be a few people who remember Hump. He's too big to forget."

"Give me some names."

"A waitress named Truckee. She talked to us at the bar before Marcy arrived. That was before eight. About eight we took a table. The waitress... I don't know her name... had short dark hair, long legs and a little mole on her upper lip."

"You started eating at eight? You sure of that?"

I nodded.

The phone buzzed. Bowser talked for a few seconds. Mainly he listened. He hung up and looked at me. "A lawyer out there says he represents Evans."

"I called him," I said.

He let out a short, angry hiss of breath. "You sandbag people when you get a chance, don't you?"

I stood up. Art followed me to the door. I'd swung it open before Bowser called out.

"I want a word with you, Art."

I waited in the hallway. Art came out three or four minutes later. He was sweating. "This better be the truth. I gave him my word he could believe you."

"It's gospel," I said.

"He's going to do some checking. I gave him Marcy's number at work. I think we can count on him springing Hump."

"Fine with me."

"He wants to talk to you." Art nodded at the closed door.

"What about?"

"A question or two."

I told him to introduce himself to James Fitch in the lobby. I'd be out as soon as Bowser finished with me. He left and I went back into the office. I didn't sit down.

"Tell me about the scratches on Evans' hands."

I told him all of it. The pool and the one-dollar rip-off and the check Hump had taken as security for the hundred Joe

Bottoms owed him. And I told him about the fight in the parking lot behind Hump's apartment.

He didn't make notes. He didn't nod. Just those tired, red eyes fixed on me. When I stopped talking, he said, "People have killed for a hundred dollars. Hell, they kill over a bottle of rotgut wine."

"Not Hump," I said. "He might knock out a couple of Bottoms' teeth. He might pass out some lumps. That's as far as he'd go."

"The check … you got it?"

I shook my head.

"The two in the parking lot didn't get it?"

"No."

Bowser fumbled with a crushed cigarette package. He tore the top off. It was empty. I passed him a Pall Mall. "The check business bothers you, Hardman?"

"Some."

He got the Pall Mall burning. "I've got to check out that part of it."

I nodded.

"Evans didn't mention the check," Bowser said.

"Can't blame him. He's not in the business of tying himself in a Christmas package for you."

Bowser pushed back his chair and stood up. There were a dozen or so angry words tap-dancing on the tip of his tongue. He closed his teeth over them and I followed <u>him</u> from the office and down the hallway to the jail lobby. James Fitch was on the bench next to Art. When he saw me, he uncrossed a leg and pushed himself up. I shook my head at him before he could gear up his pitch to Bowser.

Bowser hadn't swallowed those words yet. He swung away from me as though he wasn't with me. I stopped next to Fitch. Art edged in close and said, "If this is done, I need some sleep."

At the window Bowser tapped on the glass. The fat cop leaned in. "Bring Evans up," Bowser said.

I tipped my head at Art. That's what I'd been waiting for. "I'll call you in a day or so." Art nodded at Fitch and had a few words with Bowser before he left. Bowser stood with an elbow on the window ledge, face away from us, for the ten minutes it took to bring Hump from the cell. I think I figured him pretty well. He'd chewed and swallowed the dozen words and they gave him stomach burn. And he wasn't quite sure, if he talked to me, that he wouldn't cough up a few of those soured words.

The door to the left of the cage and window opened and Hump walked out. Another time he'd have been angry. In an hour he might be. This time all I could see was relief. He was glad to be getting out.

Bowser met him. Fitch touched my arm and we hurried over and arrived in time to hear Bowser ask if Hump had gotten his things back. Hump said that he had.

"I'll need that check," Bowser said.

Hump tilted his head past Bowser. I met his eyes and nodded. Hump bent over, lifted his right trouser leg, and dug down into the elastic part of the knee-length sock. He straightened up and passed the folded check to Bowser.

Bowser took his time reading it.

Fitch cleared his throat. "I assume that Mr. Evans is free to go."

"You the lawyer?" Bowser hadn't lifted his head from the check.

Fitch said that he was.

"He's free for now. We'll check out the girl who's supposed to have been with these two and we'll check the waitresses at the restaurant."

"It's straight," I said.

He folded the check and walked away without looking back at us.

In the parking lot, next to Fitch's blue Duster, I stopped long enough to push a hundred in cash on him. He protested some that he hadn't really done anything. The protest was weak and soft in the center, as if he really needed the money. I told him to think of it as a down payment on a job that wasn't over yet. That if he'd take the money, I wouldn't feel bad about calling him at 3 A.M. if the police made another surprise visit.

Fitch drove off. I stood around while Hump took about twenty deep breaths. "God, that place stinks in there."

I drove him to his apartment. I made coffee and read the morning paper. He stayed under the shower for what seemed just on this side of an hour. Even after that, drinking the coffee I'd made and scrambling half a dozen eggs, he said that he hadn't washed it away. The stink was buried far back in his nose and he hadn't been able to reach it.

Two days. Bowser didn't call. Art Maloney dropped by for a free beer and remained long enough to say that the times at The Brothers Two had checked out. Hump was clear, unless the pissing witness had his times messed up.

The Bottoms killing dropped off the blank end of the paper altogether. It hadn't been front-page and now it wasn't news at all. So much for that dumb life.

The third morning I awoke to the sound of rain. It was a hell of a storm. I rolled around and enjoyed that sound for an hour or so before I got up and opened the blinds. The leaves, the ones that hadn't fallen yet, looked like wet dark leather.

I walked barefooted into the kitchen and put on the coffee water. I switched on the radio. I didn't remember moving the dial but now it was on WPLO and Rex Allen, Jr., was singing about "Lying in my arms I find that you've been lying in my arms." It didn't quite fit the way I felt. Rainy days got to me. I wanted to be in some sweet woman's arms, one that was telling me the truth.

I'd had one sip of the instant coffee when my muted doorbell rang. It might have been ringing longer. After Rex Allen, Jr., there'd been Merle Haggard and Dolly Parton and Emmylou Harris and all of it was so sad and unhappy that my feeling about the rain changed and it wasn't loving anymore. It was a red-neck hurt.

I unlocked the front door and Hump pushed his way in. He stood just inside the door and shook the rain from his coat as a dog sheds water. I was about to close the door when another man trotted up the steps and sprinted into the living room. This man wasn't wearing a raincoat and I could see the rain smears and dots on his expensive suit jacket. The suit looked tailored and it looked to be about four hundred dollars' worth of cloth.

I put this man's age at about fifty. His face was sleek and round and his head was bald in the center. The hair fringe was brown streaked with gray. He wasn't wearing a hat and I could see, close up, that the top of his head was oily and drops of rain skated on the oil.

"You got coffee, Jim?" Hump dumped his raincoat over the back of the stuffed chair and headed for the kitchen before I could answer. At the kitchen door, as an afterthought, he turned and said, "This is Frank Temple."

I blinked at him.

"You know, the check."

It still didn't mean anything.

"The Frank Temple Construction Company," Hump said.

I had it then. I stuck out a hand. The one he offered me was soft and pampered. Maybe he knew the impression that the hand gave me. I'd decided just to touch the hand and withdraw mine. At the last moment he tightened his grip. He let me see the strength under the softness and then released the hand and stepped around me.

"It's good to know you, Mr. Hardman. Your friend has been telling me about you."

"Friend?" I looked at Hump. We laughed at the same time. Maybe it was the surprise. Nobody ever said that about us. To Marcy, we were Huck and Nigger Jim. To some of the blacks on the street, I was Hump's winter shadow, that kind of thing. What the red-necks thought about my relationship with Hump, I hadn't heard any of that recently. But I could guess.

Temple didn't understand. He looked confused and then he corrected himself. "Associate?"

"That's close." I waved him into the kitchen and caught Hump's wink. He was feeling his jolly for some reason. That was good. Bottoms and the rip-off were off in the background somewhere, put aside, and he appeared to have his balance back.

Hump filled the kettle and put it on the burner. I cleared an end of the table and nodded Temple toward it. After he was seated, I got down two cups and spooned in instant. That done, I got the quart of milk from the refrigerator. Before I put it in the center of the table, I opened the spout and sniffed at it. Sour. I poured it down the drain and rinsed the carton before I tossed it in the trash.

"I hope everybody takes the coffee black," I said.

"Black is fine." Temple replaced a handkerchief in his jacket breast pocket. The top of his head wasn't damp anymore and I knew he'd blotted it.

I sat across from him and looked at his hands. He placed them palm down on the table top. I could see the thick, black wire hair on his wrists where the cuffs had pulled away. "Tell me what brings you out on a wet day like this, Mr. Temple."

"Call me Frank," he said.

I nodded. "In that case, I'm Jim."

"Two days ago I received a call from a policeman here in town."

"Bowser," Hump said.

"I believe that was his name." Temple nodded. "It is not surprising that a check written on my company had found its way this far south. My company does business worldwide. I'd rather not give exact figures but the cash flow in my kind of business is considerable. Even with the recession this year growth has been acceptable."

I looked at Hump. I had the feeling he'd heard some of this earlier. Temple had paused. I realized he expected me to say something. "Stop me if I head in the wrong direction," I said. "What you're saying is that a two-thousand-dollar check written on your company wouldn't ordinarily bring you down to Atlanta."

"That's true."

"What changed all that?"

The kettle hissed. Hump poured the water into the three cups. He handed the cups around and sat down to my left.

"First of all, it was the matter of the check itself. When Mr. Bowser called, my secretary took the number from the check." He reached into his right, side jacket pocket and brought out a notebook. "That check is numbered 223455." Temple closed the notebook and placed it on the table in front of him. "And she made a notation of which account, which bank, the check was drawn on. Under usual circumstances it might have been a week before we'd have looked into the matter of this check. At the time it seemed to be a favor we were doing for the police down here."

"A part of Bowser's investigation?"

"Yes. That was how I saw it. But later that afternoon, I had a call from First Federal of Boston. The bank informed me that my account was overdrawn. That didn't seem to be possible. Though our figures were not exact we should have had a balance of almost nine hundred thousand."

I could see the edges of the puzzle. "Why aren't your figures exact?"

"I wondered if you'd ask," Temple said. "About two weeks ago there was a fire at our main office. The master computer tapes, the ones that recorded all the checks written in the last six months, were destroyed. That same fire burned up a check-writing machine and spread to the storeroom where the stock of blank checks was kept."

"You didn't consider arson?"

"Not at the time. Both the fire department and the insurance company investigations seemed to point to a hot plate that had been left burning after hours, a unit that was used by the office staff to heat water for tea or instant coffee."

That was likely. A good torch would make it look that way. Without some indicators, either increased coverage or business problems, there was no reason to suspect arson. "And you didn't keep a copy of those computer tapes at another location?"

"What they call son and grandson tapes?" He shook his head. "Banks usually do this. They have more to lose than a private company. We'd never had a fire and there was no reason to believe we'd have one."

"So, you weren't sure what checks had been written?"

"Not to the penny. But we could estimate on the basis of other peak months."

I sipped at my coffee. "But it wouldn't be anything like nine hundred thousand?"

"Not a quarter of that," Temple said.

I did those figures in my head. It was a healthy take. I pushed that aside and went back to the puzzle. I had the feeling that Temple was testing me, waiting to see if I saw the full shape of it. "Where does the check Joe Bottoms had fit in?"

Temple smiled. I knew then I'd passed the test. Or a part of the test. I decided I might as well make the leap over the gap. Either I'd prove something or I'd splatter on the rocks.

"The check to Bottoms was written on a different bank."

Temple nodded. "That's the frightening part of i

CHAPTER FIVE

"**C**lose the account down," I said.

"It's not that simple." Temple carried his cup to the sink and rinsed it out. For a moment I thought he'd ask for another cup, but I saw the decision against it. It was a godawful coffee. "Until we've done a bit of accounting it's hard to know exactly what the take from the First Federal of Boston is. It might be as high as six hundred and fifty thousand. We're fairly certain that this amount was drawn out in five checks. Checks that were written on our computer and authorized on our check writer. The largest check was for almost two hundred thousand and the smallest was for fifty-five thousand."

"Out of one bank?"

"That's another reason why I'm in Georgia. Do you know a town named Tiflon?"

I nodded. It was a town of about thirty thousand up near the South Carolina border. On weekends,, the farmers came to town and the population went up to sixty thousand or so.

"The five large checks went through the Citizens and Farmers Bank in Tiflon."

"I know a lawyer moved there a few years ..."

A short, sharp motion of his hand stopped me. "That's not my main concern. The bank in Tiflon and what happened there is a matter for the federal government and the bonding companies. It might be in the courts for years."

I found my smokes on the kitchen counter next to the radio. I took my time lighting one. Maybe it was just the way his mind jumped around. I was having trouble following him. All right. Back to the original problem. The two-thousand-dollar check.

"In a rip-off like this," I said, "it's modest and a waste of time to go to all that trouble and write a two-thousand-dollar check."

"Exactly."

"In the other operation the smallest check was for fifty-five thousand. Why two thousand this time?"

Temple waited. He was going to let me play out my string. I turned to Hump. A shake of his head meant that he wasn't going to be any help.

"The other bank the two-thousand-dollar check was drawn against...?"

"Bay City National," Temple said.

"No phony checks have been presented for payment yet?"

"Not yet."

I nodded. "And you have a feeling that the scam is over, that there is a very good chance that they've packed it in?"

"The timing is bad," Temple said. "A man bright enough to set up this operation would be bright enough to know that we're alerted now. If they were going to gut both accounts, it would have happened by now."

"But you need to be sure."

"Let me put it this way." He leaned forward and placed all his weight on his hands and pushed himself to his feet. "I spent twenty years building up this company. I've been taken, I've been made a fool of. When the word of this gets out, it's going to hurt the company. The bonding company will try to prove that we didn't exercise the proper precautions. All that. Fine. I can weather that. The real damage will be to the reputation of the management. I can handle that part, if I have to fire everybody from the steno pool up until I lean the bloody ax against my door and start over. And in two or three years, the case will be out of court and I can start rebuilding."

"You've lost me."

"I want to be sure that another rash of bogus checks doesn't get presented…"

"Close the Bay City National account."

"That is the one thing I won't do."

His temper flared at me. It burned me and I felt like backing away from him. I wanted to tell him to take his problems somewhere else.

"There is no way I can deny that I've been taken for more than half a million dollars. That's common knowledge. It will be in the newspapers in the next day or two. But I will be goddamned if I will admit that someone…"

"Could try to take you for a million or a million and a half?"

He nodded.

"That could be expensive pride," I said. I felt childish, as childish as he was. He was locked in and now I was baiting him. I said, "Back in a minute," and I left the kitchen and went into the bathroom. I ran water in the basin and ducked my face in it a couple of times. Not that it really did any good. But I wrote *Be Calm* on the blackboard two hundred times and dried my face and returned to the kitchen.

"There had to be an inside man," I said.

Temple reached into his breast pocket and brought out a small photo. It was about the size of a passport snapshot and there was the mark of the paper clip all down the left side of it. "Eric Pender. He was with the company for eleven years. Harvard Business. Good family. A model employee."

I looked at the photograph. It was a narrow dour face, thin lips and neat black hair. Dark-rimmed glasses covered stunned, inward-looking eyes. I passed the photo to Hump.

"Married?" Hump asked after a slow look.

"No. Eric lived with and took care of his mother until she died back in the summer."

"All this talk," I said, "so I've got to guess he dropped over the edge somewhere."

"What?"

"Eric hauled ass," I said.

"Eleven … no, twelve days ago, Eric asked for and got a week of vacation. An aunt in Denver was ill and he was the last of the family. It was not the best time. We were still trying to deal with the problems that the fire had caused. Still, it seemed necessary. At the end of the week he called and said that the aunt had died and that he needed two or three days to handle the funeral and close out her affairs."

"And when the overdraft showed up?"

"We tried to contact him at the address he'd given us in Denver. There was, of course, no such address."

"Figures," I said. I drew the photo toward me and gave it another look. "Can I keep this?"

He said I could. There were other copies.

"Odd you'd come to us," I said. "There are other private agencies that specialize in this kind of hunt-and-find."

I hadn't seen him take it out. The first time I saw the checkbook he lifted his hand and opened it. He unclipped a fountain pen and wrote for a few seconds. "It's not odd at all when you consider the value I place on results. Without knowing anything about this business, you've recovered a check worth two thousand dollars. That impressed me. I have better hopes for the results now that you have some understanding of the matter."

"You don't know anything about us," I said.

"I know the worst."

"Bowser?"

"The same. He said you two have an old whore's past and future. Nothing at all." Temple capped the pen and clipped it to his shirt pocket. "He said more than that."

That was to be expected.

Temple tore off the check and passed it to me. I read it. Two thousand dollars. I passed it on to Hump.

"I like to make up my own mind," Temple said.

"You want us to find those checks?"

"Or I want your firm assurance that there are no more checks. One or the other."

I lit another smoke and looked at Hump. Hump passed the check back to me. I could keep it or return it. That was up to me.

"Are you interested?" Temple asked.

I anchored the check to the kitchen table with the sugar dish. "This buys you a week. After that we decide where we are and if it's worth going on."

Temple agreed.

I was still barefooted. I stood in the doorway and watched Temple do a lumbering sprint toward the rented LTD parked behind my Ford in the driveway. Temple was halfway to the LTD when the engine turned over and the windshield wipers moved. The other windows were fogged and I couldn't see the man inside. If it was a man.

I closed the door and went into the kitchen. "The other person in the LTD ... ?"

"His driver or his male secretary or whatever," Hump said.

"That's money," I said.

Hump opened the refrigerator and got out a can of Bud. "It too early for you?"

I shook my head. "But I can't drink it in the shower."

"Maybe you can't ..." he said.

After the shower, I dressed in my best dark brown suit and a white shirt. I knotted on a conservative tie and got my raincoat from the closet. I dropped the coat over the back of the kitchen chair and looked in the refrigerator. There wasn't anything to drink in there but soured orange juice and beer.

"Bottoms is all we've got," I said.

"A look in the apartment?"

"If we can." I put the other cups in the sink and cleared the table. "I think we showed a lot of restraint. Neither of us said anything about that sheaf of checks Bottoms had the other night. If it was a sheaf in that envelope."

"More than one," Hump said.

"At least that." I struggled into my raincoat.

Hump seemed to notice the suit and the tie for the first time. "You all dressed up for some reason?"

"Some scam or other if I need it," I said.

I parked across the street from the duplex on St. Charles. Hump stayed in the car. I trotted across the street and long-jumped the flooded gutter. I stopped on the walk and looked up the drive. There was a blue VW far up the drive beside the house. I ran up the walk and stopped on the porch long enough to stamp my feet and try to shake some of the rain off my shoes.

I could see light beyond the blinds in the apartment next to the one where Joe Bottoms had lived. Pasted to the mailbox beside the door was a business card with the previous address blacked out with a few careless pen strokes. MARY SUE BASCUM.

I touched the buzzer. While I waited, I dug the badly crumpled card out of my wallet. The card identified me as an insurance agent with Nationwide. The card was so dog-eared that, one time when I'd been at Marcy's, I'd ironed the back of it with her steam iron.

Two locks. I heard both of them pulled back and the rattle of the door chain when it was attached. The door opened about two inches. "What do you want?"

The smell of her first. The scent of bath oil and the stifling cloud of dusting powder. I had more trouble with powder than with perfume or cologne. "It's about Mr. Joseph Bottoms."

"You must not read the paper," she said. "He's dead."

I angled to the left a few inches so that I could see her. I still couldn't see much. What I could see of her face led me to believe that she was in her early thirties, that she was slender, and that her blond hair was worn in those freak little curls.

I passed her the Nationwide card. I waited while she read it. I could see one eye and when she lowered the eyelid I could see some blue or blue-green makeup on it.

"He was insured with your company?"

"That's right. For more than five years."

"What do you want of me?"

"The beneficiary is an aunt in Detroit. We've been in touch with her and she's given us authorization to pick up his copy of the policy."

"There's no trick in this?"

"Of course not," I said. "It's only a formality."

"And this isn't some way of cheating...?"

I gave her my best disarming smile and just in case that wasn't good enough I threw in a boyish shake of my head. "If I find the policy, I'll be happy to give you a receipt for it." A beat. "Of course, this assumes that you have a key to the apartment."

"The rental agent, Mr. Borman, left a key with me last night. He said some family might be coming by for his things. I didn't know they had to come all the way from Detroit."

"I'm only interested in his copy of the policy."

"And you won't leave before..." She broke it off. "I have to make sure that you don't take anything out of the apartment."

"I'll wait for you," I said.

She closed the door. She returned about half a minute later and passed me a key on a tag through the opening. "I'll be over as soon as I've finished dressing."

"I'll wait for you."

The door closed. I heard the locks slide home. I quick-walked for the Bottoms half of the duplex. I didn't know how much time I had. I'd have to use what there was. I unlocked the door and went in. I hit the light switch on the way by and headed straight for the closet. I stood in the closet opening and played it back through my mind. Joe Bottoms had stood where I was now. He'd reached up with his right hand … up and to the right. I got on my tiptoes and ran my hand the length of the top shelf. I came away with nothing but dust. The dust fell on me in swirls. I stepped away, coughed, and moved on to the clothing. I patted down each shirt, each pair of trousers, each jacket.

Zero. I turned away. The chest of drawers. I went through that next. The top drawer held socks, T-shirts, and boxer shorts. The middle drawer showed neatly stacked shirts. The bottom one contained half a dozen sweaters. Off to the right, under a blue cardigan I found a neat stack of letters held together by a rubber band. A flip through these. All from the same girl in Greensboro, North Carolina. Edna Reese. All with a dormitory address at UNC-G. Probably his love life.

One eye on the closed door. I didn't know how long I had. Maybe a few more minutes. Maybe no time at all. The hurry was in me. I sprinted for the bathroom. Not in the medicine cabinet. Shaving gear and one sad unopened three-pack of Trojans.

The kitchen. Rattling through the battered collection of plates and stainless steel that came with the apartment. Two saucepans and one skillet. Nothing. I whirled and looked at the bed. It was still unmade. I was about to head there. I could check under the mattress and inside the pillowcases. Just on impulse, out of no more than my usual curiosity, I jerked open the door to the small refrigerator and looked inside. A carton of eggs, some bacon, almost half a gallon of orange juice. I was closing the door when something caught my eye. I leaned over and pulled out the clear plastic vegetable crisper. There it was. The envelope. Right on top of a browning half head of lettuce.

It had the slime feel to it. Holding it, I jammed the crisper shut with my right foot and slammed the refrigerator door. Flap sealed. I tore away the end and looked inside. It wasn't the thick sheaf of checks I'd expected. Four or five. I didn't have time to spread them out and total them. I unbuttoned my shirt right at my navel. I worked the envelope in and past my side, until it fitted into the small of my back. It rested there, long and thin and flat and cold as an ice cube.

I sat on the edge of the bed and waited for the woman next door to arrive. She'd dressed in a plum-colored pantsuit and a yellow slicker and rain hat. "Did you find it?"

"No sign of the policy," I said. At least that much was true. I hadn't found any kind of policy. "But we'll pay the claim. There won't be any trouble about that."

An abstract nod. A border of those blond curls bounced like spring wire. "I guess he wasn't expecting anyone to see the apartment."

"I guess not."

She gave the room one last sweep with her eyes. "You through here?"

I said I was. She waited on the porch while I switched off the lights and locked the door. I returned the key to her and followed her across the porch to her door. "Did you know him well?"

"Just to speak to in passing. He tried to come on but I put him off. Those young types don't interest me." Her eyes brushed me, read all there was, and went blank. I wasn't her type either. "He was awfully young."

"All of us were at one time," I said.

I could almost feel her heart stop. A deep breath and it was past and she'd decided I was talking about myself. Thirty or so was still young. Over forty was next door to dead.

"He have any friends? People you saw him with?"

A bad move. Instead of my two steps to the front and three to the side I'd stepped directly on her big toe. "Why do you ask?"

"I'm still thinking about the policy. He might have left his papers with a friend."

It didn't satisfy her.

"Or maybe he had a safety-deposit box."

Confusion. She couldn't hold suspicion and one reasonable thought in her head at the same time. "He had some visitors now and then. Once or twice they had loud arguments late at night."

"You see them?"

"I was in bed. I wasn't about to get out of bed and look at them when they left."

"Male voices?"

She nodded. "And one of them, from his voice, I'd say he was black."

That would fit. The black in the parking lot perhaps.

I thanked her and watched her enter her apartment and close and lock the door behind her. I was in the middle of the street, getting wet and not liking it, when I realized she hadn't given me my Nationwide Insurance card back. Shit. Now I'd have to have another batch printed up.

It was a late lunch. Frank Temple, Hump, and I were in the Polaris Room, the bubble-topped restaurant and lounge high above the Regency. We'd told the hostess we'd be ordering lunch and we'd been given a table next to the window. The Room turned slowly, one full circuit about every hour, and we sat and watched the city under construction. The drinks came. Vodka martinis all the way around. Temple had a sip of his before he said, "I'd like to see what you've found."

"That's why I'm here." I reached into my raincoat and brought out the envelope. I placed it on the tablecloth next to his elbow. I didn't have to read the bad news with him. I'd let Hump do the driving across town. It had given me time to study the checks a number of times. All were written on the Bay City National Bank and, discounting the odd cents involved, the five checks totaled $65,000. The payee, on each check, was left blank and the date hadn't been typed in.

"One theory went out the window," Temple said. He returned the checks to the envelope and left it in front of him. "Counting the check the police have, this second rip-off is headed toward seventy thousand and we don't know if this is the end."

"Notice the sequence?"

He had. The check we'd taken from Joe Bottoms had been numbered 223455. The five I'd found in the vegetable crisper had followed that one. 223456 through 223460.

"A block of six checks," I said. "And there are more out there somewhere."

"You sure?"

I nodded at Hump. He'd been closer to Joe Bottoms that night in the apartment. He gave his estimate of the envelope that night and the way it was now. "It might have been four or five times as many that night," Hump said.

Near the end of it, Temple lifted his drink. He looked out the window. We were reflected in the mirror-like panels of the Coastal States Building. Hump finished and lifted an eyebrow at me. I waited.

"You could have told me this earlier," Temple said.

"And disappointed you if I didn't find anything?"

"It might have changed my thinking."

"No," I said, "nothing would have changed that."

I watched the corners of his mouth relax. "Was I that overbearing?"

"Enough," I said. "Enough so that I fell back on something an old scam man told me once."

"Which was?"

"That you don't tell anybody everything you know."

Temple laughed. It was shocking. It was the first time I'd heard him laugh. Maybe, without thinking about it on any conscious level, I'd decided that he couldn't.

"Another drink?" Temple nodded at his empty.

I said, "Why not?"

One of the waitresses with the long lean legs the Polaris management seemed to prefer passed. I turned and watched her. After she'd gone by, I found myself staring into the eyes of a man seated at one of the inside tier of tables. His table was parallel to ours. A tulip glass of white wine was on the table in front of him. Then I remembered him. He'd been near us when we'd met Temple in the Regency lobby and he'd drifted onto the same elevator, just two steps behind us the whole way. While I stared at him his eyes edged past me and centered on Frank Temple.

I touched Temple on the arm and tilted my head toward the man. "He yours?"

Temple didn't look around. "He's my associate."

I gave the man another hard look. He looked hard-ass. A bodyguard. He had a lean hard body under a blue Brooks Brothers suit that would blend into any crowd or any kind of woodwork. A square jaw with a deep cleft in it. A lightning bolt of a scar with its point buried in his left eyebrow.

"A gun?"

"Not exactly." He spread his hands. "You don't know the construction business up north, out in the Midwest. Rackets have a way of wanting a finger in everything. Sometimes it gets rough. Tip makes sure that nobody gets rough with me."

The man he'd called Tip must have known we were talking about him. He placed an elbow on the chair back and turned until we'd locked eyes. His had a kind of high fever burn to them. Without looking away, he brought the glass to his mouth and let about half a teaspoon of the wine wet his tongue. At that rate, in an hour, he still wouldn't finish a single glass. That was part of the business.

"He carrying?"

"When he needs to," Temple said.

Tip's coat was loose but I thought I could detect a bulge at his right hip. "How'd he get it past the X-ray machines?"

"You have a lot of questions, Mr. Hardman."

"Call it a natural need to know," I said.

"You don't," he said. "You make a call. Someone here in Atlanta meets the flight. You make an exchange in the airport restroom. And on the way out the exchange is made the other way."

"You know a lot about how it's done. Things an ordinary businessman wouldn't know."

"It's not that complex. What I do is hire the best man I can find for a job. He makes his own arrangements. I merely observe them." He picked up the envelope with the checks in it. He stored it away in his inside breast pocket. "I haven't asked about your methods either. I've assumed you know what you're doing."

Hump grinned at me. "That's some assumption."

"You mean he doesn't?"

"He don't tap-dance good," Hump said. "But he seems to stumble in the right direction most of the time."

"That is a special talent," Temple said. He opened his menu. I swung my head around just in time to see that Tip had received the message. He'd opened his menu a split second after Temple had. Yes, we were having lunch.

Over lunch I made my argument one more time: that he close the Bay City National account. He heard me out, his head tipped over some kind of crab meat on English muffins dish. When I let it sputter to an end, he lifted his head and wiped his mouth with a napkin.

"In one week," he said.

"In a week," I said, "two or three hundred thousand dollars' worth of those checks could…"

"Not if you find them first," he said.

"That's a weight to put on my back."

His nod meant, yes, that is true. And his face was so bleak that I began to wonder if he'd be understanding if I failed. It wasn't a nice thought.

We rode the open glass elevator down to the lobby. We crossed from the express elevator to the ones that would take him up to his room. He'd said he would be checking out within the hour.

"I'll leave it in your hands then," he said.

"I'll need a way to reach you."

Temple dug out a leather card case and slid out one of the cards. He turned it and wrote an area code and a phone number. He passed the card to me. "You can reach me at that number any hour of the day or night."

I placed the card in my pocket without looking at it.

"I won't be there. It is a kind of answering service. You leave a number and I'll call you back within the hour."

One of the elevators opened. Temple and Tip started for it with a crowd of other guests. Temple stopped and came back. Tip followed him. The elevator closed and moved upward.

"I don't think I've said how pleased I am with the work so far. I'm even considering another way of paying you. We could call it an incentive plan. I may pay you a percentage of the face value of the checks you recover."

"Ten per cent?"

He shook that off. "Perhaps five."

Another elevator opened. Temple and Tip were the only people waiting. Temple stepped on first and Tip followed. Tip turned and blocked him from view. Temple leaned around him and waved as the glassed-in unit swung up and out of sight.

"Ten per cent would be something," Hump said. We'd left the lobby and walked outside. The heavy rain had stopped. It was only mist now but there was a coming chill to the afternoon. The wind down Peachtree had the smell of fall in it.

"But five is better than nothing."

All the pretty ladies on Peachtree were wearing their raincoats. It was a disappointing walk to the Davison parking deck. Downtown Atlanta spoiled you.

It got so you expected wonderful girl sights every time you passed Peachtree Center.

CHAPTER SIX

"In a vegetable crisper?"

I nodded. Marcy and I were having dinner at the Peking Taste at Peachtree and Sixth. It was northern Chinese food and the sour and hot soup, the slow burn of that, hadn't prepared me for the sauce that came with the pork dumplings. That sauce, sesame oil with fresh-ground red pepper stirred in, was liquid fire. One taste and I grabbed the water glass and sucked on ice.

"Why there?"

I woo-wooed a couple of times. The burn didn't go away. "Just a guess. Our man, Bottoms, was in trouble. He couldn't account for the one check Hump had taken from him. Maybe he decided to tell whoever it was that Hump had taken six checks. It gave him a nest egg and, if he got caught, he couldn't be any more dead. Though I don't think he thought it would go that far. And if Hump denied that he had the other five checks, who'd believe him?"

"But a vegetable crisper?"

"Best hiding place in the world," I said. "Who looks in the rotten lettuce?"

"You did," Marcy said.

"An accident," I said. "It's part of some research I'm doing. It's for a book I'm going to do someday."

"About what?"

"Strange things I have found in refrigerators in furnished apartments."

Before the main course, I headed for the bathroom. The Peking Taste is in the front corner of the Peachtree Manor Hotel.

To get to the bathroom you have to cross the lobby and take the elevator down to the underground level where there are a couple of bars. As soon as I got out of the elevator, just as the doors opened, a blond hooker bumped into me getting on. She said she was sorry and the elevator doors closed on her. I went on to the bathroom. Out in the hallway I buzzed for the elevator. When it arrived, the same blond hooker bumped into me getting off. Again, an apology and this time a money look.

Well, all days don't work out one hundred per cent. The morning and the afternoon had been fairly good. The evening had to be mixed.

After midnight. I couldn't sleep. I tried not to roll around. On the pillow next to me, Marcy bubble snored away. Loose and relaxed and all the things I wasn't.

My head was too full.

All that had happened, bright and clear, and every time I tried to decide what came next, the fog and the dark and the cold wind. Black tunnels and mazes and brick walls that didn't have gates or archways.

At one-thirty, I eased out of bed and headed for the kitchen. The floor was cold. That was because of the cold snap that followed the heavy rain. It would last two or three days and then the false spring would return. Sometimes, in Atlanta, the lasting cold weather didn't come in until late in December.

I got down the dusty bottle of Armagnac. It was about half full, and I hadn't thought about it since the winter before. I had one slow shot and I found a box of tea bags and made myself a cup of hot tea to sip along with the second shot.

Another hour, and about two inches gone from the Armagnac bottle, and I'd had one decent thought. At least, if it didn't lead anywhere, it would fill up the better part of an afternoon.

I licked the edge of the glass, cut off the lights in the kitchen, and crawled back into the bed. One touch from my cold feet and Marcy opened her eyes and blinked at me. "You bastard."

"Cold feet, warm heart," I said.

She tucked her feet away from me and closed her eyes again. The Armagnac worked on me and the warmth rocked me and I reached out and caught Marcy's hand and leaped over the dark edge about one step behind her.

Bad morning. Sand and grit in the corners of my eyes. An Armagnac belch caught halfway down my throat. The first swallow of coffee dislodged it. There.

A note from Marcy pinned to the table by the Armagnac bottle: *Is that what cold feet mean? I thought it was poor circulation in old men.*

At one, Hump came by for me and we went on a search for Bill Heffner. It was two-thirty before we found him. It was walk around and ask and buy a drink or two. Finally, a bone and skin woman in a red wig In Pete's Place looked up from her draft long enough to say, "That mouse dick son of a bitch is where he belongs."

"Where's that?"

"Union Mission and you can tell him hello from Martha."

I said that I would and I dropped a couple of ones on the bartender to fill her glass a few times.

The Union Mission is just off Peachtree, a scar on the landscape, a place where the winos and the lost ones live. Maybe we should have looked there first. All the stories we'd heard pointed him in that direction. I guess I had to believe he had too much pride to fall quite that far. If he'd gone down the rung then there must have been some straight truth in the words we'd picked up. Word that Bill had broken down the middle.

Ten years ago, he'd been one of the best scam men in the southeast. He ran a lot of the old scams but when he ran one there was always one new touch that put some shine on it. And, in his time, he'd invented ones that younger men, not half as good as he was, were still polishing up for one new score. When I'd first met him, he was on his way up. He was doing a diamond ring version of the old pigeon drop. Instead of the envelope you "found" stuffed with money in the middle of three or four greedy witnesses Bill used a five-carat diamond. And he'd done the bank examiner for a lot of little old ladies and a hundred others. It was high living and the best of times.

Until he lost his nerve. It was a matter of stolen securities and he'd set up the deal well and he was loose and easy until he realized he'd sandwiched himself between the Dixie Mafia and a ruthless man whose weapons company in Florida was in trouble with the Feds. Either way he worked it, somebody was going to be mad with him and when the money was ready to be counted he backed away. He didn't make the meet. After that he couldn't take candy from children.

Hump parked at the lot on the corner of Peachtree and Ellis. We walked the block over to the Mission. It was windy downtown but there weren't any high buildings to channel the wind where we were going and the sun seemed to perch right over us. That accounted for the row of tired men on the walk in front of the Mission. Winos, like houseplants, always turn to face the sun.

I recognized Bill with the first look. Maybe the wine had him now, and maybe he'd lost his nerve, but there was a hopeful neatness about him. His shoes, cracked uppers and all, had been given some kind of polish and his trousers and his windbreaker had been clean a day or two before. And he'd shaved earlier in the day. There was a cut on his chin. Either the razor had been dull or he'd been shaky.

He'd been heavier the last time I'd seen him. Six feet tall and he'd weighed about two-ten then. Now he might have weighed one-seventy soaking wet. Hard living on the street had taken that high-living double chin away. He was fifty now and he looked every day of it.

I looked past him after I saw him read me. I gave each man a brief Stare. While I was doing this, Hump stood at a distance and puffed at a smoke. Finally, as though I'd decided something, I moved close to Bill.

"You want a couple of hours of work?"

He stood up slowly, careful with old muscles. "Doing what?"

"Yard work," I said. "Two an hour."

He hesitated. He weighed it as if he wasn't sure. A black off to his left stood up.

"If he don't want the work, I do."

"He asked me first," Bill said. It was easy. It wasn't angry. Just a fact.

"If he don't want it," the black said.

"I'm your man," Bill said.

We walked back toward the parking lot. Bill was in the middle. We were half a block from the Mission before Bill lifted his head and winked at me. "Hardman, I hope you don't really think I'm going to rake your fucking leaves for you."

"No way," I said.

"But it's a job?"

"Money in it," I said. "My time's worth something. So's yours."

Bill got into the back seat. Hump drove. I turned and put an elbow on the seat back. Bill wouldn't meet my eyes. He was looking down at his hands and watching them shake.

"You need a drink, Bill?"

He nodded, eyes closed. I told Hump to find the closest wine and beer store.

Bill said, "It's easy enough to fight it when you know you don't have the chance of a drink, but when it's possible ..."

Hump did a few turns. We ended up at a liquor store near Georgia Baptist Hospital. I pushed open the door. "What are you drinking, Bill?"

"White port."

In the store, I headed straight for the cooler. I found a quart of white port and carried it over to the counter. The clerk behind the register looked at the port and back at me. I guess I didn't quite fit the image yet.

Bill's hands were shaking. I tore off the seal and uncapped it for him. After I passed it back to him, Hump pulled away and headed for my house. I looked straight ahead while Bill had his first three or four drags at the bottle. I counted them off in my mind. When I turned, he was smiling.

"It didn't have to be chilled," he said.

"White wine's always chilled," I said.

"Not on the street."

By the time we were seated at my kitchen table, Bill had poured back two thirds of the quart of wine. I realized my estimate had been a bottle or two short. If the mind picking took more than five minutes, he'd be looking at an empty.

While Hump opened a couple of beers, I had a look in my pantry. I found three bottles I'd put away. One was a Marquisat white burgundy I was saving for the next time I boiled a few pounds of shrimp. The other two were American wines. In my rating scale, I liked the Almadén chablis less than the Inglenook burgundy so I dusted that one off and put it in the refrigerator. If Bill didn't get that far, I could always have it with supper.

Bill had lost the shakes. And he didn't show the drunk that almost a quart of wine would put on me. "What's it all about, Hardman?"

"It's some kind of check swindle." I took a big swallow of the Bud. "Big company up north. Lot of cash flow. Somebody on the inside ran some checks through the computer. Checks on two different accounts at two banks. Ran the checks through a check writer and got the authorizing signature on them."

"That's halfway home," Bill said. He lifted the quart bottle and let a cupful run down his throat. I knew then he'd been watching when I put the chablis in the refrigerator. "You want to know how you could turn that paper into spending cash?"

"That's it. You hear anything on the street?"

"If it's going on right now, it wouldn't be on the street. That could be dangerous. And, anyway, I don't walk around in the right circles now." He gripped the neck of the bottle and tilted it back until the last drop ran out. When he tapped the bottle on the table, I put my beer aside and got the chablis and the corkscrew. He watched patiently while I worked the cork free. "The amount. Five or six figures?"

"Six and rising," I said. "It might go as high as seven."

He held the bottle away from him and read the label. He didn't taste it right away. "Say I was running this, I see it two ways."

I waited. Hump lit one of my smokes and tipped back his chair.

"I'd split the checks up four or five ways. I'd use either one good man or maybe two. I'd dress them in four-hundred-dollar suits and ninety-dollar shoes. The whole successful young businessman thing. Not too mod, not too conservative. I'd take a couple of days and I'd open new accounts in four or five different banks. These could be company accounts. Development corporations or real estate. I'd start the accounts with sizable deposits, one or two of the big checks. Enough to make an impression. And when I talked, I'd make it soft but big. This deal or that one. And in the next few days, I'd deposit more to each of the accounts. I'd make them seem busy. Each day or so another check to the account. At the end of seven or eight days the first big deposit should have cleared. By then I'd have charmed myself a branch manager and maybe a teller. And then I'd start moving money back and forth between the four or five different banks and each time some of the cash would stick to my fingers. I'd be sucking some of the funds out."

"Big amounts of cash?"

"Sure. If the scam men were good. I could do it." He lifted the chablis bottle and let some trickle down his throat. "Of course, all this assumes that the back door is covered. That somebody up at that northern company handles those checks when they come in."

Or that an arson's been arranged.

"Checks would be flying from account to account, so fast nobody'd know exactly what was going on. And in about a week or ten days, after I started draining it off, they'd find there was two hundred left in each of the accounts. The rest would be in twenties and packed away in a suitcase."

"Any problems with this method?"

"None that couldn't be handled if you figured all the traps ahead of time. What could go wrong. What to do when something slips and the red light goes on."

"It seems too easy," I said.

"Easy? Who said easy? No, it's possible. Damned possible. And what makes it possible is that banks are run by greedy little men. Maybe they don't have the guts but they understand a hustle. And envy. Lord, the envy. The branch manager is sitting there and watching a man his age play with big amounts of money and he's thinking that with some luck he could be doing the same. And when the scam man leans over and says that he needs twenty thousand in twenties to ice a deal he knows the deal is probably rank but he knows the profits will probably be high. And he goes over and gets together the twenty thousand and wishes the scam man luck."

I finished the beer and tossed it in the trash can. "There have to be problems."

"All right. First of all, the way I've set it up, you've got to deal with four or five branch managers. Maybe one of them doesn't want to play the right brand of helpful ball. One, just one, can screw it up."

"So, what's the better way?"

He lifted the bottle and sucked on it and his eyes were closed for a long moment. When he took the bottle away, he was grinning. "I would buy myself a banker. Hell, I'd buy myself a whole fucking bank."

We dropped Bill on Peachtree a couple of blocks from the Union Mission. He'd asked to be dropped there. He had a bright new twenty in his pocket and he didn't seem to be in any hurry to join the others in that sun spot.

That twenty was the hope of a fuzzy drunken warm and the way I saw it he wasn't going to share the better part of it with anybody.

CHAPTER SEVEN

I put in a call to the number Frank Temple had given me. Dialing the number, I flipped the card and looked at the fancy engraving job on the front. It was simple enough: *Frank Regent Temple* in raised black script and a number. No address. The number, of course, was not the same as the number he'd written on the back.

It was six when I placed the call. A man who sounded as though he had a breathing problem, a broken nose or something like that, answered. When I gave him my name, he said he'd have the call returned as soon as he could.

It was supper time in the living room. On the way home, I'd made a wide loop and we'd bought out a part of the deli counter at Cloudt's. I'd brought lox and pastrami and corned beef. There'd been a loaf of good dark bread and a jar of hot mustard. While I was on the phone, Hump'd started on the goodies. He'd made himself a corned beef that looked like a catcher's mitt.

"That Bill..."

"Bothers you, huh?" I stopped in the kitchen doorway. "He used to be good."

"His head still works."

"Primed by two bottles," I said.

"You're hard on the man. Ever have any drunks in your family?"

"Some." I went into the kitchen and laid out lox and a block of cream cheese and a sliced pickle. To that I added a couple of slices of black bread and a bottle of Bud. "Had an uncle when I was a kid. Used to breathe pure Four Roses on me. All the time singing about how he'd be glad when I was dead, you rascal you. And he'd rub his whiskers on my face."

"That explains you and drunks."

I spread some cream cheese on a hunk of bread and layered on the lox and some pickles. "Look, Hump, I understand it. The shakes got to you. You felt sorry for him and later you realized he hadn't quite pickled the rest of his brain. Now you want to help him get straight again. But let me tell you. It ain't that easy. You help him start walking on two feet rather than four and the first thing he'll do is put on a clean suit, get him some fake identification, and go over and run a scam on your Aunt Edna."

"Which scam?"

"The bank examiner one. He'd probably find out from you that your Aunt Edna has a big savings account at First Georgia. He'd go to her, charm her a bit, show her those fake credentials, and ask her help in a very, very secret matter. The way he'd tell it they suspect that one of the tellers is dishonest. He'd even have one picked out. Name and description. Now, the way of checking whether this teller is dishonest is for your Aunt Edna to take all her money out of the savings account. He'll have some reasonable way of explaining how this will reveal the crooked employee. He'll be so convincing that your Aunt Edna will go to the bank. While she's drawing out the money, she'll see Bill over talking to the branch manager. Really all Bill's doing is asking how you apply for a charge card. Bill shows up at your aunt's house an hour or two later. It's probably after banking hours. He's very pleased, very grateful. They've caught the crooked teller. And they'll talk some more and he'll never come right out and say anything but your Aunt Edna will suddenly realize that she has got twenty thousand dollars in cash in the house. And she gets so concerned about the money that Bill will offer, even outside of banking hours, to take that money and deposit it for her. He'll even give her an official-looking receipt. And that's the last your Aunt Edna will see of the money or Bill."

"One thing wrong with that story," Hump said. He tossed a crust of bread in the ash tray. "Where'd my Aunt Edna get twenty thousand dollars?"

The phone rang while I was choking on the lox.

"Mr. Hardman?"

"That was fast."

"I assume there's been some progress."

"Nothing to speak of."

"But you called," he said.

"It's about the original rip-off. There's been nothing in the papers here yet. I need to know how it was handled."

"I don't have all the details yet. All I know is that all the checks went through the Citizens and Farmers Bank in Tiflon."

"One account, one bank?"

"I don't even know that for sure," Temple said.

"My nose is against a stone wall," I said. "Nowhere to go from this end. I'm going to Tiflon in the morning. I told you I know a lawyer there. I'll muck around in the scam there and see if it leads me somewhere."

"They're in Atlanta," he said.

"As of a few nights ago. Lord, they could be in South Dakota by now."

"Go ahead but time's running out."

I said I knew that and I'd be in touch in a day or two. He broke the connection. I sat on the edge of the bed and lit a smoke and had a few drags. Maybe it wasn't such a bad idea after all. When I returned to the living room, Hump was playing flip-flip with the TV set. All he could find was local news.

"How strong do you feel that about Bill Heffner?"

He switched the TV set off. "Why?"

"My question first."

"Strong enough," he said.

"I've been thinking. Maybe we could use an expert. Somebody who'd know the possibilities, what the moves might be in a game like that."

"Bill?"

"If you'll nursemaid him."

"That's some deal."

"You're the one who wants to rehabilitate him so that he can run scams on all your aunts and uncles."

"All that tough talking didn't fool me," Hump said.

"You think you can find him?"

Hump pulled back his sleeve cuff and glanced at his watch. "In a couple of hours."

"Huh?"

"That twenty still has some dollar bills left in it."

Hump left a bit after eight. After he left, I made a call to Marcy and told her I'd be going out of town for two or three days. It hit some possessive chord in her. She said she'd be right over.

"No, let's meet for a drink. You can pick the bar."

"Why can't I come over?"

I could feel the stiffness and the suspicion. "All right, come on over."

"Why didn't you want me to … ?"

"I said you could come over, didn't I?"

"Is there some reason … ?"

"Hump's turning my house into a rehabilitation center for winos."

"A what?"

"I'll explain it."

I did. She picked 590 West, the bar on the top of Stouffer's Inn on West Peachtree. Over some drinks, I told her about Bill, about Hump's interest in him, and the way I thought I might be able to use him in the job we were doing.

Marcy, I think, didn't find much amusement in it. She might do social work for a living but she had a way of locking it in her desk at five in the afternoon.

The living room smelled of vomit. The lights were out and I did some careful walking until I got the lights on. There wasn't anything on the floor or the chairs or sofa. I checked my watch. It was eleven thirty-four or so.

Light spilled out of the kitchen. I went in that direction. Just before I reached the doorway, I heard Bill Heffner mumble, "Fuck you, you black son of a bitch."

"Names, names," Hump said.

I leaned on the doorframe. The vomit was in the kitchen sink. A darkish border was hardening on the front edge. Bill's back was to me. Hump had a stranglehold on him, a lump of forearm muscle under his chin. There was a coffee cup in Hump's free hand. He was pouring black coffee down Bill's throat as fast as it would go. Bill was sweating and his skin was the color of an eggshell. His hair, sparse in the center and needing a trim, was matted and damp.

I shouldn't have spoken. Hump saw me and if I'd waited a moment his brief, short nod would have stopped me. "How's it going?"

Bill jerked his head. The cup tipped against his chin and coffee poured down his shirtfront. "Hardman, you tell this nigger here…"

"Tell him yourself."

"This is kidnapping."

"Maybe you like that life," Hump said.

"It's my life."

"You told me you'd give it a couple of days," Hump said.

"You didn't tell me…"

His mouth was open. Hump raised the cup and braced it against Bill's lower lip. Bill gagged. I backed out of the doorway and went to bed.

※ ※ ※

I didn't sleep well. Maybe I should have stayed and helped. The second time I had that thought I threw it away. They'd been doing well until I'd walked in. Without me there it was one on one and Bill didn't have anyone to do his abuse act for.

The voices ran on and on. And then, after some twilight sleep, the silence awoke me. I fumbled for my watch on the night table. It was two-eighteen. I got out of bed and eased the door to the living room open.

In the spill of light from the kitchen I could see Bill on the opened-out sofa. He was wrapped in a couple of blankets, directly centered on the sofa. He was exhausted, worn out. Motionless.

I found Hump in the kitchen. He was bent over a plastic trash bag, stuffing Bill's clothing into it. "You don't have to whisper," Hump said. "He wouldn't hear a shotgun if it went off next to his ear."

"It worth it?" I got down two glasses and the remainder of the Armagnac.

"Ask me in a day or two."

The stench was bad. I had a belt of the Armagnac and placed the other glass and the bottle on the kitchen table. I ran some water in the sink. Hump had done a half-assed job of cleaning. I gave it another polish. "You have experience at this?"

"Saw this John Wayne movie once."

I sat at the table and sipped the brandy. Hump wrapped a tie around the trash bag and carried it outside. When he came back, he washed his hands and poured himself some of the Armagnac. After a swallow he said, "The truth is I had this Uncle Tolliver. That was when I was a kid. Good man. Big dude. But he had this drinking problem. Every three months, right on the tick of the clock, he'd go on a toot. The size of the toot depended on a lot of things. It depended on what cash he had to start with and what he could steal. When it started running down, we'd have to put him back together so he could go and look for another job."

"Was it this bad?"

"This?" Hump laughed. "This ain't bad at all. With Uncle Tolliver you had to dodge fists and elbows."

I offered to spell him but he shook that off. He'd started it and he'd finish it. He'd sleep in the stuffed chair for what was left of the night. But he said he needed a shower. I sat in the kitchen and had another drink. After a time, listening to the shower, I carried my drink in and stared down at Bill Heffner.

He hadn't moved. He could have been dead. Only a low nasal wheeze said it was otherwise.

❧   ❧   ❧

I folded the blankets and closed the sofa. I worked the sports page out of the *Constitution* and made a pretense of reading it. I wasn't. There was too much going on in the kitchen.

Bill shouted that he wanted his clothes.

Hump said that he'd buy him some new ones after breakfast.

Bill said he didn't want any fucking breakfast. He wanted a drink.

"Eat your breakfast," Hump said, "and you can have one beer."

"I don't want a goddam beer."

Hump said that he'd need Bill's sizes. Underwear, shirts, socks, shoes, and suit, the trouser length.

It went on and on. Hump browbeating and promising, Bill slowly being dragged along by him. Hump got the sizes. A few seconds later Hump leaned through the doorway. "Want some coffee, Jim?"

That was my cue. I could enter the kitchen.

When I told him my interest in Tiflon, he'd said I was in luck. He was handling a legal matter for a retired army captain named Morris who'd been working at the Citizens and Farmers Bank at the time of the rip-off. He'd call Morris and have him stand by. Morris owed him a favor anyway.

Van's directions got us to his office without much trouble. Find the front of the courthouse. Drive around the right side of the courthouse, go one half block, and watch for a street that intersected. That was Law Range.

It was a narrow street, still paved with brick. Long flat two-story buildings flanked the street. Lawyers' signs, about a dozen of them, wagged about in a stiff wind. Van Green's sign was the newest, the paint not weathered or chipped yet.

Up a dark staircase. The wooden steps were grooved and dished by God knows how many boots and shoes. There were two rooms to the office suite. The front room and its desk for a receptionist were empty. The door to the inner office was cracked an inch or two. As soon as we reached the top of the stairs Van swung that door wide open and whooped and made a run for me.

That was all right. He'd always been impulsive. I'd known him since he'd been working about five jobs and going to John Marshall Law School. That's the little yellow building on Forrest Avenue. It wasn't sanctioned by any bar association. There was, however, a Georgia law that went back to the times when a young lawyer read the law with an older lawyer. It didn't matter where you got your knowledge as long as you passed the bar examination. After that, you were as much a lawyer as anybody who went to the University of Georgia or one of the fancy out-of-state schools.

I caught Van by the shoulders so he couldn't hug me. I patted him on the back and turned him and did the introductions. He'd met Hump a time or two before. He shook Bill's hand and waved us into the inner office. It was dank and a little chilled. A portable electric heater guttered away in one corner.

Van has an odd face. It takes time to get used to it. I think it must have been some kind of deformity from birth: he doesn't seem to have cheekbones. Instead they're concave. And his nose is huge and tipped back so that you always feel you're staring into nostril openings about the size of quarters.

The inner office smelled of dust. Plastic wrappings on the desk held the bread crust from his lunch sandwich. A large bottle of grape soda made a damp circle on the new blotter.

Van leaned on the desk and pulled the telephone toward him. "You still want to talk to Captain Morris?"

I said I did.

While he made the call, I leaned close to Hump and Bill. "Hungry?"

"I could eat," Hump said.

"You and Bill have something and bring me back a sandwich and something to drink."

Van finished his call. "Morris'll be here in half an hour."

"A cafe around here?"

"Frank's, on the street behind the courthouse."

"They sell beer?"

Van nodded. I watched Bill out of the corner of my eye. He'd been getting steadier and steadier as the morning went on. Lunch might be the test. That one beer with his meal would have to last him until supper.

I heard them go down the stairs. The downstairs door closed behind them. I placed a chair at the side of the desk and sat down. "What happened at the Citizens and Farmers Bank?"

"Captain Morris knows more about it than I do."

"For starters I'll settle for the little you know."

"It's not much," he said.

"Come on, Van. This is a small town. It took more than two weeks to run this swindle. You'd hear most of it."

"Tidbits."

"Whatever," I said.

He settled into his chair behind the desk. "It started about three weeks ago. Two men come to town in a black 1975 Continental and they take the best suite at the Planters Hotel. It's all first-class, the clothes and the luggage. The next morning, early, they're out looking for office space. They're picky, hard to please. A whole morning and nothing they see interests them. After lunch at the hotel, they stop by the bank. They have a long talk with the president of the bank, J. B. Southern. And they open an account in the name of Apex Investments."

"Not very original."

"Maybe they didn't plan to be. Anyway, they deposit a check drawn on the Temple Construction Company in Boston. That check is in the amount of about one hundred and fifty thousand dollars. That's a big deposit for this town and I guess you could say the red carpet, such as it is, was rolled out for them. Later that day, after seeing some more real estate they settle for an office suite over on H Street. It's an old building and there's the question of knocking out a wall or two to make the rooms big enough. The owner, Jess Carter, agrees to that and he agrees to have the outside of the building sandblasted. They sign a one-year lease and Carter gets a check written on an Atlanta bank for one month's rent and a deposit. Apex Investments allows as how they're going to do their own remodeling on the inside of the suite. Sure enough, the next day they show up at Liz Hoffman's. Liz is the only person in town calls herself an interior decorator." Van lit a cigarette and blew a puff at me. "Liz is also one fine piece of ass. I think she learned that at some art school in New York. Anyway, she's hired to do some preliminary designs. And after they leave her, there's a visit to Arch Ford, who sells office furniture. What they want is all top-drawer. They do some looking about in books and they place an order with Arch. Desks and chairs and a conference table that seats ten and matching chairs for that. Arch ain't talking about it now, but I heard the order ran to somewhere between twelve and fifteen thousand. That's about half a year's income for Arch and he promises to get that order off right away and he promises delivery in two to three weeks."

"Nice people," I said. "I can see what they were doing for the economy."

"Oh, lord, how they shook it up. And later that same day they stopped by the bank and deposited another check. This one is for two hundred thousand or so."

"Another Temple Construction Company check?"

"What else? They stay another night at the hotel and they tell the manager they want to keep the suite while they're out of town for three or four days. They'd like to leave some things there. Of course that's fine with the manager. He's been hearing tales about some high spending. And that noon, just before they leave town, they deposit another check. Fifty-five thousand dollars."

"That's a bit more than four hundred thousand," I said.

"And that's about all I know. The next ten or twelve days, they're in and out of town. They're still picky. Liz Hoffman's design is rejected but they give her a small retainer and she goes back to the drawing board. All that work she's doing has about five or six men thinking about sleeping with their wives again. And Jess Carter has a crew of carpenters knocking out walls and he brings a sandblasting crew in all the way from Atlanta. Only the best is good enough for him now. The town's all excited. It's about to become a boom town. And then, before anybody realizes what happened, it's over. The two men leave town tor what is supposed to be another two- or three-day trip and they never come back."

"With a suitcase of money?"

"They did carry at least one suitcase with them," Van said. He stubbed out his cigarette. "And now the blight's hit the town. That big shipment of furniture arrived the other day and Arch don't know what to do with it. Jess Carter's got a building with a new-looking outside and some walls knocked out inside and he's expecting a big bill from that sandblasting company in Atlanta. Liz Hoffman finished her new design. She says it's the best thing she ever did, only she don't know where to send it. The only good thing I can report is that Liz ain't wearing underwear anymore."

"You see the two men?"

"A time or two just in passing."

"Give me a description."

Van pushed back his chair and stood up. He fiddled with the cord to the blinds behind the desk. They opened and showed a gray fall day. "The older one gave his name as Edmund Frost. He was about fifty. Weighed about a hundred and ninety, about five-ten. Silver-gray hair. A good tan. Round pudgy face like a baby. Wore a big diamond pinkie ring. He gave out he was president of the company."

"The other one?"

"The younger one said his name was Richard Hart. Six-one or so. Lean. Dark hair. Long jagged face. Wore a bushy mustache. He was supposed to be treasurer."

"Age?"

"Late thirties. Maybe forty at the most."

"Wear glasses?"

"Hart? No."

I brought the photo of Eric Pender from my jacket pocket. He was the man who'd worked in Frank Temple's main office in the accounting department. The one who'd disappeared while he was supposed to be at the deathbed of an aunt in Denver. I passed the photo to Van. He held it in the light from the window.

"I can't be sure." He gave it another long look. "Without the glasses and with a mustache added on it might be."

I saw that he'd run down. He seemed to be waiting for Captain Morris. I led the talk off to other things. The Atlanta he'd known when he was there, what his prospects were in Tiflon.

"It takes time for a town to accept an outsider," he said.

"Unless he carries big checks," I said.

"That would help," he said. There was a beat. "Friendship aside, I'll be putting in a bill to you, Jim."

I nodded. "And "I'll pay it." And I'd find a way to pass that expense on to Frank Temple.

Even without the background information about Morris, I'd have guessed that he was a retired or passed-over army officer. It was partly the way he carried himself. The ramrod back, the way he moved his arms, the almost strut and march that was his walk. His shoes were light brown chukka boots and they seemed to have a spit shine. The tan twill trousers might have once been part of his uniform. Or perhaps he preferred that cloth and cut after his military service.

It was a weathered face with a ruddy cast to it. His sandy red hair had been carefully combed and arranged to mask a bald spot. Square blocky hands with cleaned and buffed nails rested on his knees. As he talked, listening to him, I saw beyond the stiffness and the military carriage. There was something soft and defeated about him, a pent-up wronged sense of himself.

Hump and Bill sat behind me. They'd placed chairs near the door that led to the outer office. After lunch and the beer, I had the feeling that Bill was about to fall asleep.

Van started Captain Morris off. The first few minutes he seemed to be walking in Van's tracks, telling me what I'd already heard. Hump and Bill hadn't heard it so I didn't try to push him forward. I let him go at his own pace.

"I didn't like it," Morris said. "There was something odd about it. It just didn't make sense."

"Why did you feel that?" It was my question. After Van had primed the captain's pump he'd backed away and left it to me.

"It was the way Southern handled it."

I looked at Van. He said, "J. B. Southern, president of the bank."

I nodded. "How was that?"

"Like anything they wanted they could have."

"It's what banks promise on TV," I said.

"But we know better, don't we? In seven days, they deposited five checks that amounted to something in excess of six hundred and forty thousand dollars."

That was close to Frank Temple's estimate. "What bothered you?"

"How the withdrawals were handled."

"You were a teller?"

"I was head teller," Morris said. "As soon as the first check cleared, Mr. Hart gave Mr. Southern notice that he'd be drawing a hundred and fifty thousand out the next day. He wanted it in twenties."

"And you handled it."

"Mr. Southern assigned me to put the money together."

"But you didn't like it?"

"It didn't seem like good banking procedure. That much money in cash, it seemed strange. But what really bothered me was the instruction Mr. Southern gave me that I wasn't to fill out the federal form."

"Which form is that?"

"It's a regulation. It used to be ten thousand but now it's five thousand."

"What?"

"It concerns cash withdrawals. A withdrawal that large would normally be telephoned to the FBI in a matter of minutes. It's their way of keeping an eye out for kidnappings. But there's a form that has to be filled out. The government likes to keep tabs on any-one dealing in large cash amounts."

"What did Southern say?"

"He told me to forget the form. I did."

"And then?"

"The next day they drew out two hundred thousand dollars. Mr. Southern put that together himself. He didn't bother to ask me."

"Tell them about the armored car," Van said.

"Two days later," Morris said, "there was supposed to be another withdrawal. It turned out we didn't have enough cash reserve on hand to handle it. Mr. Southern made a call to Atlanta and an armored car brought in some large amount in twenties. I wasn't involved so I'm not sure how much it was. It must have been at least a hundred thousand."

"Tell them about the time you were short a few twenties," Van said.

"Once Mr. Southern had made up the package but he was short five twenties. He went around to the tellers and borrowed twenties from them to make up the proper amount."

I got a photo of Eric Pender from my pocket. I didn't show it to him. That would be later. "I understand you're no longer with the bank."

"That's true. The day after he borrowed the twenties from the tellers he fired me."

"He give a reason?"

"He said my work wasn't up to the bank's standards. I think it was because I wouldn't lend him any twenties. He asked me and I didn't even bother to look in my wallet."

Van leaned forward and placed his elbows on the desk. "Captain Morris is my client. We have a large damage suit against the bank. I'd rather we didn't talk about that aspect of the matter."

"All right." I opened my hand and flipped the photo of Eric Pender. Face up now, I passed it to Captain Morris. He cupped it in his right hand and studied it. When he passed it back to me after a minute or so his head was shaking. "It could be Hart. But I can't be sure. It could be if he'd changed to contacts and if the mustache was false. You know, nobody believes me but I'd swear his mustache wasn't real. One day, that first time they made the withdrawal, I looked at Hart and one whole side of the mustache had come unstuck. Maybe he saw the way I stared at him. He reached up and patted it back into place."

"Tell me about the other man," I said.

"Frost," Van said.

"I don't know exactly what you want to know. He did most of the talking. It was a soft, cultured voice. One with a lot of southern accent in it but more educated. It was for sure that he was running the show. One look at Hart and Hart would jump."

I repeated the description that Van had given me. Fifty, five-ten or eleven. One-ninety, tanned. Gray hair and a diamond pinkie ring. "Anything else you remember?"

"No."

"Scars, anything like that?"

"Not that I remember." He hesitated. "Yes, there was one thing I didn't even tell the police. I just remembered it. I only saw it once. It was the afternoon they opened the account. I'd brought some papers to Mr. Southern's desk. When I backed away, I looked down at the back of Edmund Frost's hand." Morris closed his eyes. I saw him spread both hands on his knees. "It was on his right hand." He opened his eyes and blinked. "It must have been a birthmark. Two small red dots that looked like a snakebite."

I heard a strangled cough behind me. I turned and saw that Bill Heffner was wide awake, leaning forward. At first, I thought he might be having some kind of attack like DT's. I met his eyes and winked.

There wasn't much more Morris could tell us. Nobody'd bothered to get the tag numbers from the black Continental. The numbers they'd put down on the hotel registration had been scrambled. It was close but no cigar when the police started checking that out. Not that it really meant much. Anyone smart enough to pull this swindle wouldn't be caught through tag numbers on a car they'd used as part of the window dressings.

The bitterness, the anger had to wear down. I listened to Morris a bit more and I gave him my best grave sympathetic look. It was the kind of coin he wanted. It satisfied him, it filled him out, and when payment was complete Van walked him down the stairs and out to his car.

As soon as they left the office, Bill jumped to his feet and did a few seconds of buck-and-wing. I must have looked at him as though he'd gone crazy. He stopped and laughed. He quick-stepped past Hump, whose face must have mirrored mine. He closed the door that led to the outer office. It was done with a stage flourish. He whirled and placed his back against the door. "I guess you're all wondering why I've asked you here."

"What the hell, Bill?" That from Hump.

"It's simple. I think I'm going to earn my pay."

"What does that mean?" I got up and pushed the chair against the desk.

"Ben Pride."

"Huh?"

Bill stretched out his right arm, the hand out, palm down. He tapped the back of the hand. "The deuce mark. I've spent all day trying to think who might be good enough to run this kind of scam and get away with it. Running it ain't that much. Getting away with it is. All that planning, all the details, the whole design. Might be ten men could do it and that deuce mark culled them for me. The man called himself Edmund Frost, that was Ben Pride."

"Who's he?"

"A legend," Bill said. "The king of them all. The bench mark you measure yourself against." A cat-eating grin. "That is, if you're in my business."

CHAPTER NINE

"I'd heard he was out of the business now," Bill said.

Van Green's return had interrupted us. We'd dropped the matter of Ben Pride and we'd talked some general nonsense until we could thank him and get away without it seeming hurried. Now we were on the road back toward Atlanta.

Hump wasn't convinced. I laid back foxy and let Hump run him. "You're sure it's this Ben Pride? Just on the basis of two little marks on the back of his hand?"

"It's more than that." Bill's voice had impatience, irritation in it. Here we'd hired him as our expert on scams and we wouldn't accept his word on anything. "One, it's the way it was set up. Going right into the company in Boston and getting those checks. There's imagination. Two. That's the attention to the small details. Leasing the office suite but going past that. Having the walls knocked out, insisting that the outside of the building be sandblasted. Hiring the interior decorator. Rejecting her first design. All that. One and two. Planning and execution. It's got Ben Pride's mark on it."

"Well…" Hump said.

Bill realized that he hadn't convinced Hump yet. "You remember the afternoon you got me from the Mission?"

"Sure." Hump put an arm on the seat back and forked a couple of fingers at me. I placed a cigarette in the fork. "You were telling us how to gut an account."

"The schoolboy ways," Bill said. "And at the end, like it was a great idea, I said the best way would be to buy yourself a banker."

"I remember," Hump said.

"That's the difference between me and Ben Pride. Ben Pride never considered any way, any choice, except the last one. He'd have leaped all the way over the other ones."

"All right." It was my turn. "Let's suppose it was Ben Pride. He's got the checks and he's got the big idea. What's his next move?"

"He'd have to find the right banker and buy his ass."

"That might be a problem," I said.

"Not for the man with the right connections."

I'd moved to the left side of the seat so I could get a better angle on Bill. The enthusiasm was speed-high. If the alcohol nerves were bothering him it didn't show.

"I don't have the connections anymore. Maybe I never had ones like Ben Pride has. Here's what I'd do if I needed to find the right banker, the one with his ass for sale. Say you've done this expense sheet in your head. So much for clothes, so much for the car, so much for living expenses, so much for leasing the offices, all that. On the sheet maybe you set aside ten per cent for the banker. Say fifty or sixty thousand. The next step is to find a banker who needs a quick tax-free fifty or sixty thousand dollars."

"Or just the greed," I said.

"Need is better," Bill said. "Need'll keep him in line. One way I'd do it. Go for somebody in a stockbroker's office. Somebody needs two or three bills. Ask the question: you know any bankers who've been taking a bath in the market? Doing a bit of speculation and having trouble coming up with the money?"

It sounded possible. I grunted agreement at him.

"Or better yet…" He put his head back and laughed. The laugh had the touch of an alcohol scream in it. Maybe he didn't know it was there. "This'll show you how Ben Pride works. He'd have made a list in his mind and the stockbroker approach would have been on the bottom. He'd have picked the right way the first time out of the gate. He'd have got him some nice clean hundred-dollar bills and he'd have checked the Sunday travel pages in the paper and he'd have written down the names and addresses of two or three travel agencies."

"He's looking for a banker who travels?"

"One who takes only certain kinds of trips. The banker who goes on junkets to Vegas."

I'd heard of those. So far, I hadn't been invited on one.

"I'd walk right in and I'd have some kind of story made up. It wouldn't have to be a story that had a lot of truth. You see, these agencies deal with some pretty rough people and some of them have to be rough enough to do some collecting. In other words, they've spent a lot of time looking at the ass of the world. So, I'd have this shit story about looking for a certain kind of banker. If the man who ran the agency didn't want to be helpful, I'd ask him what hotels he deals with in Vegas. That's where the connections come in. He'd say this hotel or that one and I'd put one of those nice clean hundreds on his desk and I'd say, make a call to Vegas, and I'd give him the name of somebody at that hotel. And I'd give him some name they knew me by out there. And he'd make the call and he'd get an okay. Then I'd put three or four more hundreds on the desk and I'd get my rundown on bankers who do junkets. How many trips this banker took, how much he played for, how much he lost, how fast he was about paying up when they got back to Georgia."

"He'd know all that?"

"He'd know everything. From the man's underwear size up. That's the way it works. He's got a dossier on that man before he ever steps on that plane for the first time. And he's got sources that Dun and Bradstreet don't have. You see, that travel agent's got to protect himself. The junket's supposed to be free. Free plane fare, free hotel rooms, all the food and drink at that hotel. All he's got to do is gamble. Once he's got there, he starts drawing on an account set up for him. It's got limits. And he can draw to that limit and sometimes past it. That depends on his credit line.

But when he gets back to Georgia that banker's got to reimburse the agent for all the chips he drew out there."

"Drawing's not the same as losing," Hump said.

"You play long enough it is. Anyway, say this banker drew up to his line and his line was twenty thousand. That hotel will know almost to the penny how much of that twenty thousand he lost. One job those people who work at the hotel have is to watch the people on junkets. That word gets to the travel agent. Banker X dropped nineteen thousand. That puts Banker X right on top of the invitation list the next time the agent makes up a junket. Two or three trips and Banker X might be a little slow coming up with the cash to reimburse the agent."

"And he's the likely sucker. You set up contact. You feel him out and if he bites at it you give him part of it. The rest is due at the end."

Bill nodded. "Hell, what's wrong with it? Those checks are good as gold. They're good as certificates of deposit or fed checks. All the banker has to do is run those checks through, pay them off, and act innocent as hell when the shit hits the walls."

Talk ran down. I put my head back. The gray fall light did funny patterns on my eyelids. In the front seat I heard low mumbling between Bill and Hump. Bill was still trying to tough it out but his strength was fading. It was a long day with nothing more than two beers to hold him up.

I was half asleep when I felt the Buick stop. I sat up and opened my eyes. Hump was out of the car going into a 7-11 store on the outskirts of Atlanta. When he came back, he carried three tall Buds. He passed one back to me. I popped the tab and had a swallow. It tasted damned good. I could only imagine how it tasted to Bill.

"You know this Ben Pride?"

Bill turned to me with the can at his mouth. He finished the swallow before he gave me his that-is-a-dumb-question look. "I never met him. Even the best day I worked I wasn't in his class."

"How do you know so much about him?"

"Rumors. Stories. Tall tales. Two con men get together over a few drinks. It starts out, did you hear what happened in San Fran? The half a mil job in Detroit? And then the Ben Pride stories pop up. The fantastic designs, the classics. The twists and turns, the brilliant new move when a scam almost went bad."

"It sounds like hero worship to me," I said.

"Call it that if you want to."

"This is going to be your year," I said.

"Huh?" The beer can rim banged against his teeth.

"You're going to meet him. This Ben Pride."

"You're kidding."

I caught Hump's eyes in the rearview mirror. "It's up to you, Bill."

Hump blinked at me in the rearview. He didn't follow me yet.

"Hump," I said, "you never played against Johnny Blood or Jim Thorpe, did you?"

"You know damned well I didn't."

"But you'd have liked to?"

"Hell, yes."

I placed the beer can between my feet and leaned forward. I put both elbows on the seat back. "That's what I want. I want to pit you against Ben Pride. I'm backing you. I want you to pull some kind of scam on the greatest scammer of them all. A scam that will pull Ben Pride into the open."

"You're not serious?"

"You better believe me," I said. "That's how you earn your midnight beer."

Hump dropped us at my place. He remained in the car while I unlocked the front door and let Bill in. Bill headed for a shower. I went back out front and leaned on Hump's car window.

"You think it's possible?"

"I wouldn't want to set the odds on this." He shook his head. "If Ben Pride's this good he'll fox Bill. That could throw him back in the gutter."

"We'll backstop him."

"One thing I can say. It's got his blood jumping. You notice how he drank that beer?"

"Like it was water." I backed away from the car. "You going to baby-sit him tonight?"

"Not tonight. I've got my own social life to think about."

"What about mine?"

"One night on, one night off. Tonight's your night."

I didn't know the first thing about baby-sitting a wino. I'd never had the lessons the way Hump had. So I did the next best thing. I acted as though he was a houseguest rather than a man with a drinking problem. I called Marcy while he was in the shower and Bill and I met her an hour later for dinner at Clarence Foster's. We waited out a line and got a table in the greenhouse part of the restaurant.

We got through number-one trap without a problem. Bill shook his head when the waiter asked if he wanted a cocktail. The next trap was the one that worried me the most. I'd ordered a bottle of a Graves to go with dinner and after I'd smelled the cork and had a taste, I allowed myself a look across the table at Bill. He'd turned his wineglass upside down.

He drank coffee with his dinner. And he was courtly and charming with Marcy. He talked about cities where he'd lived. He talked about restaurants in those cities and the dish to order in each of them. It was lively conversation and when Bill left the table for the rest room Marcy leaned over toward me and said, "Why, that man is..." And she couldn't find exactly the word to describe him.

I thought, that's a con man for you. He'll even con your best girl friend.

I left him in the living room watching TV around midnight. Not that he was really watching it. I had the feeling that only one small part of his mind was involved with the late movie.

I didn't lock the booze away or hide the wine. I wasn't going to play jailer. It was up to him what he did with himself. But I've got to admit I didn't sleep right away. I heard the TV when it went off and I heard him doing some night walking.

I awoke about eight. He was rolled up in a blanket on the sofa. He hadn't bothered to open it.

His midnight can of Bud was on the kitchen table. He'd only drunk about half of it. The ash tray next to it was overflowing with cigarette butts.

CHAPTER TEN

For breakfast Bill ate a soft scrambled egg, two pieces of toast, and a dab of grape jelly. He washed it down with two cups of coffee. Hump didn't offer him his morning beer and he didn't ask for it. I'd seen Bill's eyes drift past the refrigerator a few times. That was all. I decided that it was now to the point where he had regained some of his pride. He wasn't about to ask for that beer and Hump, reading him pretty well, wasn't going to give it to him until he asked. There wasn't anything to stop Bill from going over and getting himself a beer. Nothing but his pride. That would be admitting he still had his thirst.

"Late night, Bill?" Hump sat ass-backward in the chair, arms crossed over the back of it.

"I put in some good time."

"Anything worth talking about?"

He kept us waiting. He stacked his knife and fork on his plate and pushed it away. "I thought a lot about scams. Ones that I'd been thinking about for years and never used. I wanted a big one that might be good bait. There's one I've been saving." He patted his empty shirt pocket. I passed him my smokes. "I call it the geochemist scam. Like the rest of them it's based on good simple godless greed." He smiled and put a match to the cigarette. "And it's based on some geological theory. The first step is that heat produced by radioactivity and pressure can change the composition of earth materials. After you convince somebody of that you say something about the fact that gold-bearing earth is also usually rich in silver and platinum. We call this *rich* earth."

"That's turning a good phrase," I said.

"Now, even if this *rich* earth doesn't show a lot of gold or silver or platinum it has the possibility of bearing these minerals in larger quantities if the conditions are right. It's a matter of stepping up the process, doing in hours what it takes the earth millions and millions of years. We do this in a special oven that bombards this *rich* earth with radioactivity while exerting a million foot-pounds of pressure. The end result is that *rich* earth with only low amounts of gold, silver, and platinum comes out of the oven..."

"Almost pure gold, silver, and platinum?"

He nodded at me. "Exactly."

"Anybody believe that?"

"You'd be surprised how many people believe that science can do anything. Of course, you'd need the proper dials on the oven and you'd need a substitution tray and you'd need the right man to play Herr Doctor So-and-so. I've seen worse scams work." Another puff and Bill stubbed out his smoke. "That was supposed to be the bait. I'd get in touch with Ben Pride and lay out the scam and I'd say that I needed him for the geochemist. That it wouldn't work without him."

"And that would draw him into the open?" I carried my cup to the stove and mixed some instant powder and hot water.

Bill shook his head. "I doubt it. It might have if he needed the cash. Right now, he's fat. He's sitting on top of half a mil. The chances are, even if I knew how to reach him, the word would come back. No thanks."

"Too bad." I returned to the table and spooned some sugar into my cup.

"So, I got off that. Ben Pride's warm to hot now and he wouldn't want to do even the perfect scam this soon. If he was interested, he'd say for me to call him in a year or two. That kind of thing. So, I moved off on another track. I decided we ought to find some way to threaten him."

"I don't get it."

"Blackmail," Bill said.

"You'd have to be kidding."

"Not a bit. Here's the script. Old Bill Heffner is a down-and-out second-rate scam man. He needs a stake to get on his feet again. And he's figured out what nobody else in the whole country knows. He's picked the man who pulled off the Temple Construction Company check swindle. And because he's down and out he thinks his silence is worth about fifty thousand."

"That would get a reaction all right," I said.

"I thought it would."

"Not the one you expect," I said. "It'd cost a lot less to get you offed and that's real silence."

"It's not that big a risk. The rough way is not Ben Pride's way."

"We told you about Joe Bottoms," Hump said.

"That's not Pride. That some dogfish working around the edges."

"You want to believe that, with your life on the line?"

"It's what I know," Bill said. "For a scam man rough is on the bottom of the list. Talk and persuasion are on the top."

"Run that by another tune."

"Look at it this way. If I try to blackmail him, he won't just say yes or no to it. He'll have to see me and find out what I know and how I put it together. You see, what I can figure out somebody else can too. He'll want to know where he slipped. And if he thinks it's worth paying me off, he's going to try to persuade me to settle for less. Maybe ten thousand. Maybe five. Something that's a smaller drop out of his bucket."

"I don't know about this." I had my look at Hump. His face was screwed up. He'd been weighing the risk and I could tell he didn't like the heavy dip of the scales. "Hump?"

"Could we backstop him? A hundred per cent sure?"

"Half of that," I said. Then to Bill: "You willing?"

He laughed. It was dry, like a bark. "I'm no dumb child, Jim. If I wasn't willing, I wouldn't be talking about it."

"You got it planned?"

"I know what I need. An apartment and a phone. The apartment ought to be sort of shabby. A place a down-at-the-heels con man might live."

"That's easy enough." And I added to myself, one that can be watched and guarded twenty-four hours a day.

"Now we get to the hard part. I need a recent picture of Ben Pride."

"He's had numbers on his chest?"

"I'm not sure about that part. Maybe. Two or three years ago he got picked up on a dry well scam out in Houston."

Hump dipped his head at me. "Art?"

"That might be pushing his friendship some."

"Any other way you know?"

"Can't think of any." I let it float in my head. I'd have to find a way to talk Art into it.

Bill dipped a hand into his shirt pocket and brought out a scrap of paper. He slid it across the table to me. "It would be under one of these names."

I scanned it quickly.

Ben Pride aka Fred Maple aka Charles Benson aka William Priest aka Edward Carson

I smoothed out the paper. "That's a lot of *also known as.*"

"He might have ten more for all I know."

"That all?"

"I've got to find a way to reach Ben Pride," he said.

"Shit." I could feel it tearing apart. "If we knew that we could walk right over and ..." I stopped when I saw the got-you grin on Bill's face. "Go on, Bill."

"Ben Pride's in a hole now. He's waiting to see if the Tiflon scam gets tied to him. It does and he stays in his hole. It doesn't and he can walk out free and easy. But a man like Ben's got to have places where he can be reached and still be in his hole. So, he's got post boxes. It might be a bar in Trenton, a hotel in New

York, a pawnshop in Denver. You leave a message there, he calls and gets it and calls you. And it wouldn't do any good to lean on the man takes the messages. He won't know where Ben is. All he knows is that Ben calls every day or two."

"You know that much you got any ideas how we locate this post box?"

"Somebody with good racket connections could find it for us." Bill pushed back his chair. He carried his cup to the sink and rinsed it and placed it on the counter. Knowing we were watching him he walked to the refrigerator and swung the door open. He bent down and stared into it. About half the shelves were filled with throwaway bottles of Bud. There wasn't much else. Part of a carton of eggs, some bacon. Some wads of tinfoil that held lord knows what.

Still holding the refrigerator door open, Bill said, "This is the lousiest collection of nothing I ever saw in my life. You put some cash on me and I'll do some shopping."

No reason to walk around it. "How do you feel, Bill?"

"Better than you two think I do."

That made sense. I left them in the kitchen and went to the bedroom closet. I got down the shoe box and counted out two hundred and fifty. Hump was in the doorway when I turned around. I handed him the cash on the way by. "Find him an apartment and see about the phone. Take him by Cloudt's. Anything he wants."

"When does he move into the apartment?"

"When he needs to. Not before. It might be a few days."

"There's a place empty across the hall from me. Easy to watch. A girl lived there got busted for selling drugs."

"Not there. Somebody might remember that's where you live."

He saw the sense to that. I stood around the living room until they left. Then I went into the bedroom and dialed Art's home number. He answered it so fast I knew he was already in bed.

"You sacking in?"

"For five hours or so," he said. "Why?"

"I've got to con you into something."

"That won't be easy. I've heard all your cons."

"That's why I'm going to let you sleep now. I need the time to come up with a new one. And I want you in a good mood."

"Three this afternoon at your place," Art said. "And it better be a new one."

"I might shine up one of the old ones."

"It won't pass."

He hung up on me. My next call was the number Frank Temple had given me. The same man with the stuffed-up sound took my message. I wondered when he slept but I didn't ask.

Temple called back five minutes later. I told him that the trip to Tiflon had paid off with a name. That fox in the chicken house had three or four names and now we were trying to play a game with him. To do that we needed somebody with a hand in the rackets who'd be able to find where this man received his messages.

"A drop box?"

"I guess you could call it that. You know anybody who can work from that end?"

"One or two," he said.

"I'll need this in a day." I went into the kitchen and got the slip of paper. I read him all the aka's Ben Pride had.

"I'll try," he said.

"You find you can't, let me know. I'll have to try some other way."

Temple said he would. "If you're getting close, I'll fly down."

"Not yet." I didn't want him in the way. "I'll tell you when."

"This week's running out."

I said I knew that and he was quiet for a few seconds, waiting to see if I had anything to add. When I didn't, he said he'd get back to me and broke the connection.

⚜ ⚜ ⚜

The refrigerator didn't seem to belong to me anymore. Bill filled it with soft drinks and steaks and cheese and a couple of kinds of juice. He had to take out two six-packs of beer to make room for it all.

They had looked at two apartments. One was too shabby and the other wasn't shabby enough. After lunch I sent them off to continue the search. I didn't want them around when I had my talk with Art Maloney.

By three-ten I'd finished my pitch to him.

Art sucked on a beer and finished it about the time I ran out of words. "What's in it for me?"

I knew he didn't mean money. Some other cop and I might have read it that way. But Art was a hell of a lot more honest than the bottom row of cops I'd known while I was on the force. "The guy who killed Joe Bottoms."

"You sure?"

"Good chance," I said.

"That all?"

"One more possibility," I said. "Tied up with the same ribbon we might have the man who ran the check scam in Tiflon."

"That's a big package," he said. I passed him the list of aka's and he copied them into his notebook. "Houston, you say?"

"It's what I heard."

"There might not be a picture."

"If not, we've got a problem."

"You skated around it," Art said. "You didn't say why you need the photo."

"Caught me," I said. "The truth is I don't know. It's some con Bill Heffner's running. He hasn't even told me what he wants with it. Hell, for all I know he hasn't decided yet."

"Bill Heffner? I heard he was on the street."

"He's coming back. He's Hump's project for the year."

Art stood up and closed his notebook. "I always liked that slick son of a bitch."

"He probably loves you too," I said. That was my con for the day.

The house was on Charles Allen Drive, one of a series of wooden frame houses, relics out of some past or other. It was the area that had been taken over by the street people, the hippies, after they got pushed out of the Tenth Street haven. Now they'd moved on and the section of town was changing back. There was even a neighborhood association that was campaigning for clean streets and neat lawns and new paint jobs on the houses.

The apartment that Bill had rented was on the first floor of a house that had been renovated back in the spring or summer. It had been painted white with a dark green trim. There was the gleam of new gutters and a downspout. But nothing had been done about the high ceilings. It would be hell on the heating bill.

It was apartment 1, the first apartment on the right as you entered the downstairs hallway. The living room was the size of a postage stamp. The tired old sofa had a shine to it that meant the cloth was one strain away from letting the springs through. Straight ahead there was a kitchen and dining room combination about half the size of the living room. Off to the right was the bedroom. The bed just about filled it and the mattress was covered with a zip-on plastic sheet that crackled when you touched it. The one window had a rolled-up paper shade and no curtain. The bathroom looked like an outhouse that had been moved indoors.

I agreed it was shabby enough. A down-at-the-heels scam man might live there while he planned the score that would free him of it. It had incentive built into it.

On the way out I stopped on the porch and looked in both directions. I wanted to know the street well. If it got under way, when it got under way, somebody would be spending a lot of time in a parked car out there. I could only hope the bad weather held off as it was supposed to.

The fourth day. I ticked them off on my fingers. One day looking for Bill. The second day in Tiflon. The third day going after the pieces of the puzzle and finding the apartment. The fourth morning I wanted to sleep in. I might have if Art hadn't called.

"I'm going off shift and I've got something for you."

I said I'd put on the coffee water.

Art let himself in about twenty minutes later. When he reached the kitchen doorway he said, "If this gets back to me I swear that I will..."

He stopped and had his long look at Bill. Whatever he'd heard about Bill being on the street hadn't prepared him for what he saw. Bill had shaved and showered and he was still using the Brut as though he thought smelling good was important.

"Art, how are you?"

Bill turned from the stove where he was cooking himself a big breakfast. He looked healthy and clear-eyed and if there was a shake left in his hand it didn't show.

"You sure this is Bill Heffner?"

"You can call me William. I'm a new man." He scooped eggs and bacon into a plate and sat down.

I gave Art a cup of coffee. He pulled the cup nearer to him and dropped a 6 1/2 by 9 1/2 brown envelope next to the sugar dish. "That's your plunder, Jim, and it better not reach back to me."

I opened the clasp and drew the picture out. "Get your promises out of Bill. He's the only one knows what's going on."

It wasn't a mug shot. It was more like a candid. It had probably been taken through a two-way mirror in the interrogation room. It was either a tight bust shot or it had been trimmed to that. It matched the descriptions we'd gotten in Tiflon except for one detail. Ben Pride had been wearing his hair black in those days. I passed the photo to Bill.

"So that's how he looks?" Bill braced the photo against the sugar dish and stared at it. "Look at that baby honest face. Tell me you wouldn't buy a bridge from him."

"Maybe a used washing machine," I said.

"It's a good size," Bill said. "I won't have to have it blown up. That's one less step in the process."

"Make me feel good," Art said. "Tell me how you're going to use it."

"I'm going to make myself a Wanted poster."

"So, keep it to yourself," Art said.

"No, I really mean it." Bill replaced the picture in the envelope and started on his eggs. "And there won't be any sweat about it getting back to you. After I use it, I'm going to put it in my scrapbook."

"You keep a scrapbook?" I didn't know when to believe him.

"I'm starting one," he said.

CHAPTER ELEVEN

I was shaving when the phone rang. I gave my face a last two or three sweeps with the blade, wet the end of a towel, and caught the phone on the eighth ring. I could hear Art and Bill laughing it up in the kitchen. I hadn't known those good old days had been that funny.

It was Frank Temple. "You know what day it is?"

"I'm counting just like you are." I used the wet end of the towel to wipe away the lather. "And that's all the more reason I need a location on that drop box."

"That's why I'm calling. I had some people asking around and it wasn't easy information to get. Jackpot is a bar called Donovan's on Sixth Avenue in New York." He read me off a street number and a zip. "It turns out the bar is owned by a retired con man used to work some with Ben Pride."

"That makes the package," I said. "I'll get back to you."

"I'm coming down."

"Look, I'm not even sure this con will work. Save yourself the trip. It might be gloomy down here."

"You mean you've wasted four days on ...?"

"I hired the best I could. Like you do, right? Well, I've got to give him his run at it."

"My man, Tip, could be helpful," Temple said.

"It's not that kind of deal. I don't need any bones made or any arms broken."

"I'm flying down today."

I stood and turned. I threw the towel through the bathroom doorway. It hit the front edge of the basin and bounced back. I'd thrown it that hard. "It's your air fare and if you come down I want you to have a good vacation. Take in Stone Mountain and Six Flags but I don't want you two mixing in this. You could queer it."

"People don't talk to me that way."

"It's one or the other. You stay out or I'm out."

I waited out the silence at the other end of the line. If I hadn't had my ear close to the receiver, I might have thought he'd hung up on me. "If that's the way it has to be," he said finally, "then I'll stay out of it."

"That means Tip too."

"All right."

"And I'll need some more cash. It's spending fast."

"I'll bring some."

I waited. He didn't have any more to say. I told him to call me when he'd checked into a hotel. I'd drop by and see him then. After that, I wouldn't expect to see him until it was done.

I dropped the slip of paper with Donovan's Bar and the address on top of the brown envelope. Bill, who'd been washing dishes, dried his hands on a paper towel. He nudged the envelope until the paper slip was at an angle where he could read it. "If this is what I think it is we're in business."

"That's the last piece," I said.

Art leaned in and read over Bill's shoulder. "Of course, you're not going to tell me this either. I don't expect it, but what the hell is Donovan's Bar?"

"*The* place to drink in New York," I said.

"It's where I send the Wanted poster," Bill said.

"Shit, I need some sleep," Art said. "This ain't making sense to me."

I walked to the front door with him. "I owe you one."

"And I'll collect."

"I expect it." And I did.

Bill wanted the kitchen to himself. I wandered through now and then to make a cup of coffee. He seemed to be doing some kind of layout. He had paper and pens and a ruler. I didn't lean over his shoulder. I left him to it. I sat in the living room and read the *Constitution* page by page.

After an hour, Bill came in with a folder. He placed the folder on top of the TV set. "It's done except for one part. I need the phone number of the apartment on Charles Allen."

"Oh, shit." I'd let that slip and it might be where the whole plan fell apart. Southern Bell wasn't exactly speedy about putting in new phones. Sometimes it took a week or ten days.

"Hump's working on it," Bill said.

"How?"

"He said he knew a black beauty at the phone company."

He did. I remembered her from a time before. There'd been a lot of her to be beautiful. I think I'd said she looked like a busted bale of hay.

Around noon Hump called and read off the new number to Bill. He added that to his folder and knotted his tie and put on his suit jacket. "I'll need your car for a couple of hours and about seventy-five dollars."

I tossed him the keys and counted the seventy-five into his hand. After he drove away, I sat there and thought, yes, he is a con man. A good one. He's not exactly cured and there he is floating about in this big city with my car and a chunk of my cash.

Dumbass me. Perhaps.

That six bits would buy a lot of wine.

It looked like a parody of a Wanted poster from one of those Saturday afternoon flicks you saw as a kid. And I'd seen a lot of them. My memories went all the way back to Buck Jones and right up to Lash LaRue.

It was a good job. He'd paid high money to get the type set at one of the shops on Spring Street and he'd taken the camera-ready copy to a good print shop. The photo of Ben Pride was centered on it. Across the top the type was almost an inch high:

WANTED
FOR THE $640,000 SCAM
IN TIFLON, GA

And below the photo, in smaller type:

Ben Pride
aka Fred Maple
aka Charles Benson
aka William Priest
aka Edward Carson
aka Edmund Frost.
Contact Bill Heffner, area code 404-872-6141.

He'd only had a few copies made. I returned the poster I'd been reading to him. "You mailing this?"

"It's already mailed," Bill said. "To Ben Pride, care of Donovan's Bar."

"That ought to shake them."

He nodded. "It'll be in New York tomorrow. I sent it special delivery and every damned thing else I could think of."

"When do you expect … ?"

"It might be a day or two. It's according to Ben Pride's schedule, when he takes his messages. I'll move into the apartment tonight. I don't want to miss the call when it comes."

"You seem sure."

"He'll call."

In the late afternoon I ran him by a Kroger's where he did some basic shopping. I helped him get settled in. I was at home watching the network news when Frank Temple called to say that he'd arrived in town.

"It won't work."

This time Temple had checked in at Stouffer's Inn on West Peachtree. I met him at 590 West, the bar and restaurant on top of the building. While we waited for drinks, he passed me an envelope. The cash was in hundreds and I guessed, without counting it, that it was at least two thousand. And then, after we'd had first sips of our drinks, he'd wanted to know what the operation was.

I told him as much as I wanted him to know.

Tip sat at the table with us this time. He sat there like a brooding cloud, a harsh presence. He hadn't said a word yet and that got on my nerves.

"It might."

"I don't like *mights*."

I slugged back the rest of my J&B and water and pushed the glass toward the center of the table. I choked a word or two down and looked at the lights and the low skyline outside our side of the building. When I could talk it came out straight and level. "I don't work this way. You find him yourself."

"Even if we find this Ben Pride, how do you know he's got that group of checks?"

"I think Eric Pender is with him. I think Pride used <u>him</u> in the scam. Pender ran the machines so he'll know where the checks are."

He didn't have an argument against that. He shifted ground. "We do this together."

"No way." I tilted my head toward Tip. "He might be a professional. You're not. And I'm not sure we want the same things out of this. So, it's my way or not at all. You have fun. See the city." I stood up and nudged the chair against the table. "That's my last offer."

Temple didn't say anything. After a long wait he nodded. Next to him Tip looked at me over the rim of his glass of white wine. The fever burn was in his eyes.

"All right. That's our deal. And if I see either of you until I call you, I'll back right out of it. No matter how close we are."

I reached the elevator before I knew that Tip had followed me. I hit the button about the time Tip tapped me on the shoulder. "Yeah? What is it?" It was said harsh, hard. I didn't feel like playing.

"Your mouth is getting your ass in trouble," he said. His voice, now that I'd heard him speak, was soft, almost delicate and feminine.

"Get it on. Right now." Getting your ass beat isn't the worst disaster can happen to you. "You got something against this location?"

He was a pro. Words didn't cut him. He shook his head. "It's not the right time."

The elevator doors opened. I waited. He shook his head and backed away. I stepped into the elevator and hit the lobby button.

The doors closed and I rode the elevator down to the lobby. The heat was on in the hotel but all I could feel was the chill. It matched the cold wind that blew the length of Peachtree Street.

Hump and I started nursemaid shifts the next morning. Twelve hours on and twelve off. Hump called the quarter and took the first turn, the 8 A.M to 8 P.M.

The first stage, the way we figured it, would be in-house watching. We'd guard the warm body close up until the call came in. After that we'd change it to four-hour shifts and do our watching from a car parked across the street. Nighttime would be bad. A cold snap was heading in. And there were other dangers. A tenant in one of the nearby apartments might see us and call the police. Or the police, or routine patrols, might roust us.

It was the fifth day. Hump's shift drew nothing. Out of boredom Hump and Bill played two-handed poker for pennies. Bill won the lot and loaned Hump enough to keep him playing. By the time I relieved Hump, he'd lost about twenty dollars to Bill.

I followed Hump into the hallway and closed the door behind us. "How's Bill holding up?"

"Don't worry about him," Hump said. "But if he sucks you into playing cards with him, watch out I think the old bastard cheats."

Bill appeared to be satisfied with his twenty dollars in winnings. He didn't even mention cards. We sat in the living room and watched the flickering picture on the old set that came with the apartment. The new season had started but all the shows might have been left over from the year before. At ten-thirty I left him to the TV and stretched out on the bed. There wasn't any possibility of sleep. Every time I breathed or moved, the plastic mattress cover cracked and popped.

The phone rang a bit after eleven. I made it to the phone half a step behind Bill. He lifted the receiver and held it just far enough from his ear so that I could lean in and listen with him.

Bill said, "Hello."

The voice was flat, without much inflection. "This Bill Heffner?"

"It is. Who're you?"

"Which aka do you want?"

"The last one on the list," Bill said.

"Edmund Frost," the man said.

"That's the right one."

"I've asked around about you," the man said. "Small-time but good small-time. What I heard doesn't dovetail with this."

"It wasn't that small-time," Bill said. He was going off in the wrong direction. Here we were pulling a scam and he wanted to protest his ranking. I put a hand on his shoulder and when he looked at me, I shook my head.

"It's relative anyway," the man said. "What is it you want, Bill?"

"I've been down a few months. I need a stake."

"Down? One word I got was that you were in the bottle with the cork on tight."

"That's past," Bill said.

"Speaking of past," the man said, "blackmail is not supposed to be your best game."

"That's a strong word for it. I'd like to think of it as a loan from somebody in the same business. The first scam I run, I'll cut you in fifty-fifty on the score."

"I am not a banker." A pause. "Which reminds me. It is a fanciful idea you have. I am fairly certain that I have never been in a town named Tiflon. What part of the state ... ?"

"The Feds and the bonding company know where it is."

"That's the threat?"

"Think of it as collateral for the loan," Bill said.

"I don't think an amount was mentioned."

"Fifty thousand will bank a new scam I've developed."

"I don't care what you want it for. I don't care if you're about to donate it to one-legged orphans. That is a lot of money you are talking about."

"It's a bare minimum I can get by on."

"I haven't seen the material you mailed. It was read to me. I understand that there is a picture involved."

"A clear one," Bill said. "You hair's black but I think the real estate dealer, the interior decorator, the man who sold office furniture … all of them could identify you from it."

"Could?" The man waited. "I don't remember a picture."

"I have my sources."

"And the location of the drop?"

"The same," Bill said.

"One aspect of this bothers me. This could be a setup."

"I don't need that sort of reputation. I do need fifty thousand."

"All the same I smell a setup."

"If I sold you, who'd buy? The way you tell it no one has any link that ties you to Tiflon."

"That's true. I must say I am interested in what leads you to believe I might be involved."

"A fact here. A fact there. All well documented."

"It's all very vague," the man said.

"It should be," Bill said. "I don't believe in doing much open talking on phone lines. I understand that bored operators sometimes listen in."

"I see. You want a face-to-face with me?"

"Not at all. That's not necessary. All I want is the money."

"No," the man said. "I don't think that will work. I believe we ought to talk."

"You can't jawbone me down. Fifty is my bottom figure."

"We'll see."

"A meeting would be a mistake," Bill said. "Just send the cash. No check, please."

"I'll fly in tomorrow," the man said. "We'll have our talk and I'll decide then."

"I'm not much for talking," Bill said.

It was the way we'd plotted it. Maybe he was overplaying that part of it. But I'd told him to act as though he didn't want to try on the glass slipper. That only as a last resort would he agree to a meet.

"And I am not much for paying out fifty big ones on the basis of rumors."

"A standoff," Bill said.

"Precisely. I will need your address."

I touched Bill's shoulder. I mouthed, *not that easy.*

"You have the number," Bill said. "Call me when you get here. Or would you rather I met your plane?"

"It's an amusing idea," the man said.

"I thought it might be."

"You must take me for a fool. If I see you—and there is quite a bit of if in this—I will see you at a time and in a way that does not put me in a box. I will need your address."

Bill looked over his shoulder at me. I nodded. Bill gave him the Charles Allen address.

"If I know Atlanta your part of town is no Sandy Springs or West Paces Ferry."

"It's fine for now," Bill said.

The connection was broken.

⚜ ⚜ ⚜

Bill leaned in the kitchen doorway while I made us a couple of cups of coffee. He should have been happy. The scam had worked. It was under way. But I could read his face. He looked as if he'd just been told he had herpes simplex 2.

"Something bothering you?"

"It was too easy," he said.

"I think you handled that part of it well. It was just hard enough."

He wanted to believe me. He tried it out. "Any way for us to check if the call came from out of town?"

"Hump might work something tomorrow with the black beauty at Ma Bell's."

"Not before tomorrow?"

"If then," I said.

He took the cup I offered him and we sat in the living room and sipped the coffee. The silence and his gloom were getting to me. "Tell me what bothers you about it, Bill."

"If you dropped a hook in the water and the fish not only bit but he swam over and walked up on the ground and jumped in the creel, wouldn't that bother you?"

"Some," I said.

"Ben Pride ain't that kind of fish."

I had trouble sleeping. After the coffee I needed a drink but Hump and I had decided not to keep any at Bill's apartment. If the tension got to him, if he fell off the wagon, he'd have to brew and distill his own.

All that rolling around confused the time. I'd taken the sofa and the springs were so near the surface. I moved to avoid one and ran into two more.

Except for my movement it was still and quiet in the apartment. Now and then there'd be a feather snore from Bill. Nothing else. Then I heard the door to the hallway open and close. No, I sensed it. I didn't really hear the door at all. It was done that smoothly. I did notice a change in the sound. The texture altered. I could hear street noise for that brief time and then it was gone, chopped off.

I let the springs dig at me. Still. Not hearing the footsteps approaching the door. Rather feeling them like a shifting of weight, a changed pressure.

Someone tried the door. It was done with care. Only a faint metallic scrape. *No way, buster.* I'd locked the door myself and I'd threaded the slide bolt and attached the door chain. So much protection that I'd decided a sour, musty virgin had lived in the apartment at one time.

Knocking at the door. Firm and loud. I counted the raps and got to five before it stopped. In the bedroom the plastic sheet cracked and Bill said, "What?" and I heard his bare feet hit the floor. I reached under the sofa and grabbed the .38 P P and jack-knited off the side of the bedding. A spring clawed at me. I jerked it free and reached the bedroom doorway in time to meet Bill head on. I caught his arm and whispered, "Company."

"Who?"

"I don't know."

"Ben Pride?"

Rapping at the door. Again five times.

"I know it's him. He said ..." Bill pulled away from me.

I reached for him and missed. He stumbled toward the door.

"Is that you, Ben?"

I ran toward him. One of his hands touched the doorknob. The other worked the slide bolt. I made my low dive at him. My knees hit the floor but I reached up and caught Bill around the waist and spun him. He fell over me, sprawling, belly down.

The blast of rounds above me, so close together that I couldn't count them. Wood splinters fell on me. That was close. Close to dead. I put an arm over my face and waited. The ringing in my ears went away.

This time I heard the front door slam.

CHAPTER TWELVE

The police arrived in five minutes. I hadn't called them.

The hallway jammed with curious tenants from the other apartments and I could only guess that one of them had done the telephoning. One woman in curlers and a robe kept sniffing the gunpowder air and saying, "Disgraceful, just disgraceful."

One of the patrolmen ran them back to bed while the other listened to our story. I could see that he didn't believe it. It was, though, the only tale I'd been able to come up with in the short time I'd had.

I said that Bill and I had been drinking coffee and talking when somebody knocked at the door. We wouldn't open it and somebody had fired some shots through the door. "Some dope-crazed kid, I guess," I said.

"Robbery?"

I said I thought that was it, right on the head. Of course, all I knew about dope-crazed kids was what I read in the news-papers. On the other hand, I said, Bill had just moved in less than twenty-four hours ago and maybe somebody thought they were shooting at whoever had lived there before. It was enough to confuse their minds. The patrolmen gave it up. Nobody'd been hurt and there was still some of the dark morning left to cruise through. After telling us that a detective would be by in the next day or two to follow up, they left.

I closed the door behind them and locked it. I stopped in the kitchen doorway and looked back. Bill was measuring him-self against the jagged bullet holes. They were in a line. The first one, chest high on him, was right above the doorknob. The others, inches apart, wag-walked toward the center of the door. I'd counted four holes in all.

"You were right, Jim."

"Luck," I said.

He followed me into the kitchen. "There's a lot I don't know about this kind of business."

"The fish story of yours spooked me."

"We're even then. You almost convinced me there wasn't anything to worry about."

I put the coffee water on.

"I'm not sleepy anymore," Bill said.

I wasn't either. But coffee wasn't what I needed. I needed a stiff drink about five knuckles high.

The phone rang exactly at seven. It was three and a half hours since the try on Bill. It was three hours since the police had left. Bill and I had spent the time nodding off sitting up. It hadn't been a comfortable night.

I figured it was Hump checking in. I took the call with visions of my bed in the back of my mind. I grunted into the phone.

I knew the voice right away. The flatness, the lack of inflection. "Heffner?"

I waved the phone at Bill. He trotted over and took the receiver. "Yeah?"

I leaned in and listened.

"I understand you had some excitement this morning."

"You can call it that if you want to," Bill said. Bill looked at me. I mouthed, *be tough.*

"That solution was not my idea. The rashness of my associates ..."

"Bullshit," Bill said. "The only reason I'm here right now is that the federal building downtown isn't open yet."

"That could be a mistake."

"You made the mistake, buster."

"The stake you need ..."

"I might get it this way," Bill said. "Maybe the Feds have a finder's fee. If they don't, the bonding company might."

"That would be bad faith. We have a deal."

"Some deal."

"After I spoke to you, I asked ... my associates ... to do some checking on you. I did not ask ... for what happened."

"Easy enough to say now, when it didn't come off."

"I think I can convince you."

"That would take some doing," Bill said.

"Do you know where the Plaza drug store is?"

"I know."

"In the lot behind it, really behind the Plaza Theater ... there is a yellow 1974 Cadillac."

"The money in it?"

"Nothing that neat," the man said. "This is rather messy."

I understood it. Bill gave me a puzzled look. I nodded. *Go on.* Bill said, "You were afraid of a setup. I am too."

I knew what we'd find in the yellow Cadillac. Somebody as dogmeat. That was Ben Pride's show of good faith. And if he was willing to go to that extreme, I knew the hook was in gut-deep.

"There should be some way you can verify this without risking a setup."

I nodded at Bill.

"All right," Bill said.

"I'll call you in a couple of hours."

He broke the connection.

I got the phone from Bill and dialed the police station. I worked my way through the switchboard until I reached Art Maloney. "I've got a question. You alone?"

"Go ahead."

"Anything happen behind the Plaza Theater tonight?"

"Nothing I know of. Wait a second." He was gone for a minute or so. "A blank on that."

"Had a call," I said. "Somebody said there was a mess in a yellow 1974 Caddy parked back there."

"What kind of mess?"

"I don't want to guess," I said.

"So, this call is in the nature of an anonymous tip?"

I said that was close.

"Where'll you be?"

"The Plaza drugstore still open twenty-four hours a day?"

"As far as I know."

"I'll be at the fountain counter having breakfast."

"Be there." He hung up.

I called Hump. He said he'd be leaving in a minute or two. I told him to hurry right over. I was leaving and I'd be back soon as I could.

I didn't have to do scare stories for Bill. I stood in the hall and heard every lock put in place.

The guard had changed at the Plaza drugstore. The nightcrawlers had gone to bed or wherever they went when the sun came up. Replacing them were the blue and white collars on the way to work. I found a space at the counter and ordered eggs and bacon and toast. I had coffee shakes so I settled for a glass of milk.

I finished eating and paid my way through the turnstile. I was at the magazine shelf flipping through sports mags when Art came in. He said, "Just a second," and got himself a coffee to go. I followed him outside and stood on the walk next to the display windows.

Art had a sip of the steaming coffee. "You were right. It was a mess."

"Who?"

"We don't know yet. No identification on them."

"Them?"

"Two. One black and one white. You know them?"

A bubble broke on the top of my dull mind. "One of them wearing a hat?"

Art nodded. "A checkered Bear Bryant type. He wasn't exactly wearing it. Part of his head was in it."

"Might be the two who tried to mug Hump for the check."

Patience wasn't Art's big virtue. "What the hell is going on, Jim?"

"That picture you got for me."

"Ben Pride?"

"I think Ben Pride just put down a palace revolt."

"You think?"

"More than that," I said. "He told us where to look."

"The sheet on him. Nothing about execution-style killings in there."

"Better than half a million tax-free," I said.

"Huh?"

"Could change somebody."

Art carried the rest of his coffee to the trash receptacle next to the drugstore's front door. "Where'll you be?"

I gave him the address on Charles Allen.

One more sip of the coffee and he dropped the cup in the trash. He said he'd be there as soon as he could shake free. If he could.

"I trust that you verified it."

I heard that much and stepped away. Art leaned in and put his ear near the receiver. I went over and sat next to Hump. He looked fresh and rested. I knew I looked like the wrong end of a mule.

"I heard it was a mess," Bill said.

A pause while Bill listened.

"The price is still fifty big ones."

I looked at my watch. Nine o'clock.

"You're the one wants the meeting," Bill said. "All I want is the cash. In fact, after what happened behind the theater, I'm not sure I want to be anywhere near you."

I left the sofa and nudged Art out of the way. He'd heard enough to know the story was straight.

"... only way you'll see the money," the man said.

"All right."

"Tonight at ten I want ..."

I shook my head at Bill. "Daytime only," he said. "People get killed in the dark."

"What do you suggest?"

I'd set it up with Bill. The location and the time.

"I'll be at the Midnight Sun bar at one this afternoon."

"No," the man said.

"The reason I picked the Midnight Sun is that it's only a block from the federal building."

"You talk like you've got all the cards," the man said.

"All fifty-two," Bill said. "You see, the good faith you showed this morning put your other ball in the crack. It's murder now." He paused. "In fact, I have some trouble thinking of those killings as a show of good faith. I think you were cutting down the way you split the score."

I mouthed, *raise the money.*

"I can't be in Atlanta by one this afternoon."

"You're already here," Bill said. "And the money has just gone up to seventy-five thousand. There's more to be silent about."

"If I come ..."

"You'll come."

"... how will I know you?"

Bill gave him a rundown. Physical details. "I'll be wearing a gray suit and reading the *New York Times* sports section."

"The *New York Times* has a sports section?"

Ben Pride broke the connection.

"Boxed," Art said. He picked up the black raincoat that he wore as a light topcoat in the fall. "I don't know how I'm going to explain all this to Captain…"

"Not a box," I said. "It's going to be a box with one end open."

"What the hell does that mean?"

"Ben Pride walks in, makes his meet with Bill, and walks out again."

And then I told him the how and the why of it. It had to do with half a million in cash and a bundle of checks that hadn't been cashed yet.

I never did convince him but I turned his flank. By the time I'd drawn the layout of the underground mall at Peachtree Center and started x-ing in the spots it became a chess match for him. He couldn't resist it.

And since he'd done most of the planning, I pretended it had been his idea the whole time. Not that he bought a nickel's worth of that.

Hump said it was brilliant.

I said it was beautiful.

Bill slapped him on the back.

Art said, "Screw you, all of you." And he didn't smile.

CHAPTER THIRTEEN

By twelve-thirty, we'd built the box in the underground mall of Peachtree Center. There's an open courtyard on the street level on Peachtree Street. Up there, Hump had that end. He was seated on one of the concrete benches that surround a jumble of plants. It's girl-watching territory but, in case that didn't give him a cover, I'd set him up with a *New York Daily News* and the want ads from the *Constitution.*

Anyone entering the underground mall would pass through the street-level courtyard. Once past that point, there was a choice of two sets of escalators. It wasn't much of a choice. Both escalators dropped you in the open-air patio, a wide airy place filled with outdoor cafe metal tables and chairs. According to which escalator you took, you either turned right or left and you were at the Midnight Sun. If you continued through the patio there was a single entrance that led into the covered mall of other restaurants and shops.

The patio was my end of the box. The tables and chairs were for people who brought their own lunch or made do on the hot dogs and beverages that the Primrose stand offers.

It was a gray, chill day and I'd known there wasn't going to be much cover from other lunch-timers in the patio. I'd called Marcy and she'd agreed to meet me. She'd arrived at twenty of one and she'd made a lot out of the fact that she thought I'd invited her to lunch at the Midnight Sun. It was a misunderstanding that would cost me a sixty-dollar dinner in a week or two.

I'd selected a table off to one side, near the Primrose hot dog stand and away from the walkway that led to the covered part of the mall. My seat faced the two entrances to the Midnight Sun and, to either side, the two escalators.

Hump and I were the two open ends. If Ben Pride entered, carried out his transaction, and left by the escalator to the street level Hump would follow until we caught up. If, after leaving the Midnight Sun, Ben Pride entered the covered part of the mall Marcy and I would follow.

And in the Midnight Sun bar Bill and Art did their waiting. Art was at the back end of the bar drinking scotch and water. Bill was about center bar. He was drinking Coke and reading the front section of the *Times*. The sports section was carefully put aside for his one o'clock reading.

At ten of one, I left Marcy at the table and bought three hot dogs, one of them without onions for her, and two cups of coffee. I'd finished the first of my two and had started the second when Ben Pride walked out of the covered mall behind me. He still wore his hair the silver-gray that we'd heard about in Tiflon. His dark suit looked like about four hundred dollars worth of cloth and thread. His tie was silver-gray. His shoes were pebble-grained and English-made. He carried a thin black attache case in one hand and one of the distinctive book bags from Brentano's. So, he'd come early and browsed in the bookstore. That didn't make sense. He was too careful for that. Unless...

With his hand on the door to the Midnight Sun lounge Ben Pride turned and looked across the patio. By the time his eyes flicked to my table, I'd stuffed most of the second hot dog into my face. Mustard ran down my chin, bits of onion tumbled down my shirtfront, and Marcy, without any coaching, had her head back, laughing at me.

I think we passed muster. Ben Pride swung the bar door open and stepped inside. It was, by my watch, still two minutes until one.

I chewed and chewed and finally got the hot dog down. Marcy leaned across the table and wiped my chin with her napkin. "There, there, little baby."

"He's in the Midnight Sun," I said.

"You mean I can stop acting?"

"Eat your hot dog," I said.

She ate it delicately, quarter inch by quarter inch. No mustard ran down her chin. That was Marcy, her upbringing. She could eat spareribs without getting grease on her fingers.

Unless…

Then I saw the second man. He'd been at the hot dog stand. When he stepped away, he carried a single hot dog in his hand. He was a tall, lean man, coal-dark hair worn short. It was a long, dour face, topped by dark-rimmed glasses. He'd been looking past us, toward the covered part of the mall. Yes, to see if anyone tailed Pride. Nobody had.

Now he passed the front of the Midnight Sun and stopped at the base of the escalator to my left.

Eric Pender. It had to be.

I gathered hot dog containers and the balled-up napkins. "I've got to see Hump. Watch for Art."

I pushed back my chair and headed for the trash can at the base of the other escalator. I was a step away from the can when Eric Pender turned and stepped onto the escalator. I stuffed the trash in the can on the way by and hit the escalator running. I didn't wait for it to move me up. I ran the steps. That would be my edge if I had one. On the other escalator, hidden from me, Pender might be taking the ride, letting it move him upward to the street level.

I hit the street level. No sign of Pender. I slowed to a fast walk. Hump looked up at me. I sat down next to him and scooped up his *Daily News.* "Eric Pender's coming out now. The escalator behind us."

"Who?"

"Pender, the accountant who worked for Temple."

"I remember."

"Don't lose him but lie back."

Hump lowered the want ads and looked over his shoulder. When he turned back, he said, "I got him. He's heading for Baker Street." He got to his feet. "See you."

I kept the *Daily News* in front of my face and counted to twenty. I lowered the paper and both of them were out of sight.

Back in the patio, I bought two more cups of coffee at the Primrose stand. "Nothing yet?"

"Unless you think two men trying to pick me up is nothing."

"Any luck?"

"I told them I was waiting for dessert."

It was a hint. I crossed to the Midnight Sun Bakery and bought her a hamburger-bun-shaped éclair. While she nibbled at it, I checked my watch. Ben Pride had been in the bar for ten minutes.

Another five minutes passed before the door to the bar opened and Bill and Ben Pride came out together. They were laughing and I got a look at Bill's flushed face. Oh, shit, he'd been in the sauce. All that sauce and he'd decided to have some of it mixed in with his Coke. And Art, even if he'd known, couldn't do anything about it.

Ben Pride still carried the attaché case. The book bag was tucked under the armpit. The other hand, his left, was on Bill's shoulder. A bit of pressure and Ben Pride turned Bill toward the escalator to my left. That wasn't in the plan. Bill wasn't to leave with him. Told expressly not to.

As soon as they stepped on the escalator, backs to me, I said, "Call you later," to Marcy. I headed for the escalator to my right. I was halfway there when Art came out of the bar. I waved an arm in the direction of the escalator they'd taken. He turned that way and stopped. I knew he was counting it off in his head, letting them reach the street level.

My escalator was crowded. I couldn't run it this time. I was halfway up when I heard the woman scream. I tried to push my way up and out but a man said, "I beg your pardon," and pushed back. I didn't want to start a fight so I said, "Excuse me," and waited. I reached the street level and moved around him. My first look was toward the courtyard, toward the street. I didn't see Bill or Ben Pride anywhere. Then the woman screamed again and I ran in the direction of the other escalator.

I found Bill Heffner. He was seated, back braced against the outside of the handrail. He had both hands pressed over his chest. Art leaned over him and pulled at his hands. Off to one side, a young girl, probably a secretary on her lunch break, leaned against the wall in shock. I didn't see the attaché case. The Brentano's book bag was at Bill's feet.

Art nodded toward the street. I ran in that direction. I looked both ways. No sign of Ben Pride. I returned to the escalator well. The secretary was mumbling, "...gray-haired man said it was a heart attack and that he was going to call a doctor."

I stepped past her and leaned over Bill. His eyes were closed. Blood ran through his tightly pressed fingers.

"Ambulance is on the way," Art said.

"Bill," I said, "Bill."

He opened his eyes. "Conned me," he said.

"How?"

"Said he had a good idea about ... how to ... run the geochemist ... scam. Said he ... couldn't ... talk in the bar. Dumb ... but I knew ... you ... were watching ..."

He closed his eyes. The pain was bad.

"A knife, I think," Art said. "Just leaned on him, stuck it in him, and walked away."

I could smell the booze on Bill's breath. I straightened up. The girl said, "But it was funny."

"What was?"

"He said he was going to call a doctor but when he got to the street, he looked in both directions and a bus pulled up at the stop and he got on."

So, he hadn't planned it. Nobody planned on a bus for a getaway. He'd made the meet with the idea of paying off and he'd seen Bill with booze in him and he'd improvised. He hadn't done a make on either Art in the bar or me in the patio. And Eric Pender had been his backstop and he hadn't seen anything out of the ordinary either. Probably, if he had, he'd have looked in the bar. Going away, leaving, meant it was clear.

And Ben Pride had decided that he didn't have to pay off a scam man with a drinking problem. Also, because Bill drank, he couldn't trust him.

I could hear the ambulance siren as it came down Peachtree.

Art pulled me aside. His breath hissed at me. "Where the fuck was Hump?"

"Following Eric Pender," I said.

"You blew it," Art said.

I didn't have any answer for that. I stepped around him and looked down at Bill. He was shivering. Blood soaked the front of his trousers. I squatted and picked up the book bag from Brentano's. I tore the staple away and pulled a book out. It was *Angels: God's Secret Agents* by Billy Graham.

Bill died in the ambulance on the way to Grady Hospital.

CHAPTER FOURTEEN

I drove home in a blue funk and rage.

When the ambulance arrived, Art had shown his I.D. and we'd hopped a ride. We'd been a block away from Grady when the attendant shook out a towel and placed it over Bill's face. Done, ended.

Art and I remained on the ramp after they pushed the stretcher bed inside. He'd been rough on me and he knew it. The anger had washed away and he realized I was as hurt as he was. Maybe even more so because I'd recruited Bill into it.

"The way I see it," Art said, "Bill let the smell of alcohol get to him. After that, it was simple enough to order booze mixed with his Coke. I didn't even notice it. I had my eyes on the entrance."

"I told him. You were there. I told him not to leave the bar until ten minutes after Ben Pride did."

"Sober, I think Bill knew that. But you know how Bill felt about Pride. He was number one, the king. I couldn't hear what they talked about in the bar. From what Bill said, I think he told Pride about the geochemist scam he'd developed. My guess is Pride complimented him on it, seemed interested, and told Bill he saw an angle or two on the scam that Bill didn't. There Bill was, alcohol running strong in him, and Ben Pride, *the* Ben Pride, was going to help him and give him some ideas. No way Ben could have walked away from him."

"Scams, scams," I said. "I thought Bill was smarter than that."

"Write that on his headstone," Art said.

❖   ❖   ❖

I caught a cab that took me to the Davison deck where I'd left my car. I left Art to do his lying. *Was in the underground mall. Doing some shopping. Heard a woman scream and found a man dying on the escalator on the ground level. The witness, a Miss Sissy Jackson, said a gray-haired man. . . .*

The blue funk didn't want to leave. I found most of a bottle of J&B and had a drink. Then another. I couldn't shake it out of my head. Except for Hump's good intentions, except for my willingness to use Bill Heffner, he might still be alive. He'd be shivering in the late afternoon sun in front of the Union Mission, free and easy, his only worry the next drink of wine and how he'd get it.

"Where the hell have you been?" It was Hump. I could hear street noises in the background. I figured he was using a pay phone and he'd left the door partly open. "This is the second time I've called."

"Where're you?"

"It's been some afternoon."

"You lose him?"

"No, I'm looking at him right now. Anyway, we went to this movie. I followed him straight from Peachtree Center to the Ashley Art. Lord, that was some movie. You wouldn't believe what those boys and girls were doing to each other. One hour on the dot and he left and stood at the bus stop right outside the theater."

"You wait with him?"

"Thought that might be obvious. No, I walked down a block to the next stop, where Ivy cuts in on Peachtree. I could see him from there. I passed up the buses he did. Saw him catch a number 2. Got on myself. He was sitting up front. I did my slightly drunk nigger act and sat in back, near the rear exit door. Saw him get up just before we reached the Plaza. Got off there too. Gave him fifty yards and followed him. You know the Shady Rest? Little hotel near Manuel's Tavern?"

I said I did.

"He was in there twenty minutes. I think he was checking out. Now he's sitting out front on a bench with a big suitcase next to him. He's been there an hour. I think he's been stood up."

"Where're you now?"

"A 7-11 down the street but I'll be at the bus stop on the other side of the street from the Shady Rest when you get here."

I said I'd be there in fifteen or less.

I caught the green lights and made it in twelve. I cruised past the hotel. Eric Pender was still there. He looked grim and angry. A heavy topcoat was draped over the suitcase next to the bench. I found Hump half a block down the street on the left. He was leaning on the bus stop with his back to the Shady Rest. I waved at him and made a left turn into the seven-eleven parking lot. Hump trotted after me and slid into the passenger seat in front.

"See him? Don't he look like an orphan?"

I said that he did.

"You get Ben Pride?"

I shook my head. "Slipped us."

"How did that happen?"

"Not now." I opened the door and stepped out. "You drive."

He moved over behind the wheel. He waited until I rounded the Ford and slid into the seat next to him. "You got a script for this?"

"How about subtle kidnapping?"

"Fine."

"Around the block and pull up in front."

He gave me a sharp look. "Something's wrong."

"Later," I said.

While he did the box step that would place us on the curb next to the Shady Rest I opened the glove compartment and took out the .38 P.P. I passed it to Hump and he braced it between his left thigh and the door.

I got out, closed the door, and headed straight for Eric Pender. He looked at me. His eyes read me and flipped away. I think he believed that I'd swing aside and go into the hotel. Instead I leaned down and picked up his topcoat and the suitcase. "Ben sent me," I said.

He grabbed for the suitcase. I kept it. I quick-walked toward the car. I was a step away from the back door when he caught my arm. "How do I know...?"

"I told you. Ben sent me. There was a complication at Peachtree Center. He couldn't come."

He hesitated. I jerked my arm free. I opened the back door and tossed the topcoat and the suitcase in.

"You coming or staying?"

He leaned past me. Either he was going with me or he was reaching for his topcoat and suitcase. I didn't wait to see which it was. I put a hand on his rump and shoved him. He said, "What the hell...?"

I pushed in behind him and closed the door. While he struggled to turn toward me, I tapped Hump on the left shoulder. He passed the .38 back to me.

I held it low, on a line with his nose. "Surprise."

Hump eased away from the curb.

Pender's glasses had fallen low on his nose. He used a finger to push them back into place and blinked at me.

"Where?"

"My place," I said. I grinned at Pender. "Relax. It's not a long drive."

Eric Pender sat stiff-backed on my sofa, looking straight ahead. Hump stood over him. I squatted over the suitcase and flipped the catches. I swung the top open and dumped the contents on the floor. Nothing but clothing. I kicked those aside and stood up. I placed the suitcase on the arms of the easy chair. I found what I was looking for in the elastic pockets at the back of the suitcase. Five thick bundles of twenties and an envelope. The envelope held about a dozen checks drawn on the Temple Construction Company account at the Bay City National Bank.

I fanned the checks and waved them at Pender. "Want to explain these to me?"

He hadn't spoken since his first protest when I'd pushed him into the car. He didn't now, either. He shook his head.

I returned the checks to the envelope and tossed it in the suitcase with the bundles of twenties. "You think it's a matter of bank fraud, huh?"

He didn't answer.

"You better do another think." I went into the bedroom and dialed Art's home number. Edna answered. "I've got to speak to Art."

"He's sleeping, Jim."

"It's important, Edna."

"It better be." The rattle of the receiver as it banged on the night table and I could hear her waking him.

I said, "Art, before you start bitching, I've got Eric Pender. I'm home. You'll need a warrant. Accessory to murder."

I hung up and returned to the living room. I could see from Pender's face that he'd overheard my conversation. I could read concern and disbelief. "You don't believe it, huh?"

"I didn't have anything to do with killing Buddy and Red."

Hump grinned at me. "See? He can talk."

"You think I mean the two in the yellow Caddy?" I shook my head at him. "I mean what happened today at the Peachtree Center mall."

Hump jerked his head around at me. He was puzzled. It wasn't the way I wanted to break it to him, but I'd started and I didn't have time to walk off in a corner with him. "The killing of Bill Heffner," I said. "Ben Pride stuck a knife in him."

It happened so fast I didn't so much see it as hear it. Hump hit Eric Pender with the back of his hand. The black-rimmed glasses flew across the room and hit the wall next to the front door. Pender fell sideways and covered his face with his hands. Hump was on him. He grabbed Pender by the arms and pulled him upright. I stepped in fast and caught Hump by the shoulders. "No, Hump, it was Ben Pride."

"This bastard worked with him."

It was an effort. I felt the cords of muscle relax in Hump's shoulders. He rammed Pender into an upright position and backed away. "Bill?" He still didn't believe it.

"Stone dead," I said.

Hump shoved past me and went into the kitchen. I looked at Pender. He couldn't see well without his glasses. There was a cut on the bridge of his nose where Hump's hand had slammed the glasses against it. The cut began to bleed. Pender rubbed a hand across his nose and smeared the blood.

"Funny thing about the law," I said. "An accessory is as guilty of the crime as the one who pulls the trigger or uses the knife. You were backstopping Pride today. I'll testify to that. I saw you there."

"Scumbag," Hump said. He filled the kitchen doorway. He'd found the bottle of J&B and a glass.

"Tell me about the Bay City National checks," I said.

Pender looked down at his hands. He saw the blood for the first time and I thought he'd vomit. "He … why, he …"

"That's nothing to what he'll do if I let him."

Hump took a swallow of the J&B neat and grunted.

"If I tell you … ?"

I nodded.

Ben Pride had handpicked him. As a man at a dance picks the plain and horny girl from a crowd of fifty. All his life Eric

Pender had lived with his mother. It hadn't been much of a life. His mother dominated him and then in the summer she died and he was free but he didn't know what to do with that freedom.

He met Ben Pride in late August and for the first time he'd had his inside look at the world that money made possible. There'd been drinking and dinners and young girls. And when he had developed a taste for that life, Ben told him how he could afford it and he had listened.

He worked late some nights and one night, when he was alone in the office, he'd processed the checks drawn on the First Federal of Boston. He hadn't stopped there. The more he thought about it the more the split he'd accepted from Pride didn't please him. So he'd run off a series of smaller checks on the Bay City account. This group of checks would be his own nest egg.

"You torch it yourself?"

"No. I drew him a map of the office. I let him make a duplicate key from mine."

I believed him. Torching was not a job for beginners. "How much was the nest egg?"

"Almost two hundred thousand."

"And your split from the Tiflon score?"

"One hundred thousand," he said.

"And you were going to pass the Bay City checks yourself?"

"It seemed easy enough after you understood bank procedure."

"Through Joe Bottoms?"

Joe Bottoms was his cousin, a few times removed, on his father's side of the family. During the time in Atlanta, before he and Pride moved on to Tiflon, Pender had looked up Bottoms. Bottoms had gone in with him and he'd been given one quarter of the Bay City checks. Pender hadn't trusted Bottoms completely and he'd felt that the promise of the other checks, better money, would keep him honest.

Late in the running of the scam in Tiflon, the disaster hit. Somehow, even now he didn't know how, one of the Bay City checks turned up in the bundle Ben Pride was passing. It was a small check, only ten thousand. Ben Pride made his first guess and hit the roof. He'd roughed up Eric Pender. And with good reason. A badly run scam in Atlanta, one handled by beginners, could ruin the rest of the Tiflon one. Pender gave in and sold out his cousin, Joe Bottoms.

"I didn't think they'd hurt him."

The last weekend trip out of Tiflon, Ben Pride, not wanting to show himself, had hired two men to visit Joe Bottoms. The first tune, perhaps the one the girl next door had overheard, Bottoms convinced them that he had already deposited the checks in such and such an account. He'd been warned by the two men not to touch the account. The truth was that Bottoms had chickened out. He hadn't deposited them and he was still trying to work up his nerve.

Some discreet checking by Pride revealed that the account hadn't been opened the way Bottoms swore that it had. He sent the two men back. They visited him the day after Hump and I did. Frightened, scared by them, Bottoms told the first lie he could think of. He said that Hump Evans had taken the checks from him. The lie didn't save his life. Then the men went after Hump. When the attempt in the parking lot failed, Ben Pride called them off. The scam in Tiflon was almost over. If the checks weren't banked yet, there was no reason to believe they'd reach the Boston bank in time to arouse any suspicion. Convinced of that, Ben Pride had lost interest in the Bay City account. So, Eric Pender had kept the other $150,000 in checks, just in case he ever found a way to use them.

The rest of it we knew.

I got two glasses and poured Pender and me a drink. His hand shook so much he lost most of it on his shirtfront. After he finished, I walked him into the bathroom and watched him while he washed up. I even found a band-aid for the cut on his nose.

Art arrived a few minutes later. The warrant and the squad car were on the way.

CHAPTER FIFTEEN

I was on the back steps with Hump. The bottle of scotch, an inch or so left in it, was between us. We'd left Art talking to Eric Pender. Now we watched the dark thunderheads rolling toward us above my garden terrace. The talk about Bill was behind us. We'd kicked some gentle sand over that. Kicking sand was better than scratching sores.

Art stuck his head out the back door. "This Pender says you two kidnapped him."

"He said that?" I tapped my glass on Hump's knee. "I thought we did a citizen's arrest."

"He says you held a gun on him."

"Me?"

Hump laughed. "Him?"

"I don't even have a gun." I stood up. I brushed the seat of my pants and nudged the remainder of the bottle toward Hump. "I'd better talk to him and get it straight."

I followed Art into the living room. Eric Pender was in my easy chair now. His hands were cuffed in front of him, a concession to the fact we didn't think there was any danger left in him. The band-aid on his nose had a brown blood crust on the lower end.

"You know Ben Cooper?" I said to Pender.

"No."

"That's it." I spread my hands at Art. "He doesn't know Ben Cooper. Ain't that hell? You know him, don't you, Art? Black stud drives a Yellow cab."

Art said that he did.

"All I said to Pender was that Ben sent me. If he didn't know Ben Cooper then why the hell did he get in my car?"

Art chewed and swallowed a laugh. Pender gave it up. He lifted his cuffed hands and rubbed at his eyes. He must have felt like Alice in Wonderland.

I found a pack of smokes on top of the TV set. I let Art have one and lit us both. "What time is the flight, Eric?"

"We were taking the bus."

"All right, be a snot." I pointed a finger at the open suitcase where the envelope of checks and the bundles of twenties were. "You do a count on the cash, Art?"

"A rough one. It's between twenty and twenty-five thousand."

I blew a trail of smoke at Pender and tried on a smirk. It didn't seem to fit. "A hundred thousand was supposed to be your share of the score, right?"

Pender shrugged.

"Mister, you got jobbed. By a master at it. Not even a sixth of the total for doing more than half the work. That's short end. And he wouldn't let you run your own little swindle with the Bay City checks. Killed your cousin and got you involved in a murder this afternoon without telling you about it. What does it take to convince you?"

"You were jobbed," Art said.

"Go on and play dumb." I bent over the suitcase and plucked the envelope of checks. Art raised an eyebrow at me. "This was what my hunt was about. Ends it for me."

"Not important," Art said.

At the bedroom door I had my last blast at Pender. "If God had meant for you to act rich, dumb as you are, you'd have been born with a gold American Express card."

Art trailed me into the bedroom. I found Bill Heffner's folder and slipped one of the Wanted posters from it. "You know somebody at airport security?"

"Joe Benson."

I passed him the poster. "It's a long shot. Might be he booked his flight using one of these names."

He found the number in his notebook and dialed it. I dropped the envelope of checks on the night table and looked around. Eric Pender stood in the doorway. "Yeah?"

"It was a United flight to New York. Leaves at seven-ten tonight."

Art said, "Hold it a second, Joe."

"What name?"

"Richard Bristow for him, Ned Pendergast for me."

Art repeated the names into the phone. There was a wait while Benson checked with United. "Is that right?" Art said. Then to us: "He scratched that flight."

"See if he booked another. Probably the same name."

It was a longer wait. "Nothing with United? Well, okay, you call me…"

"He have a passport?" I asked Pender.

"Both of us did. We were flying to New York and then to …"

"London?"

Pender nodded.

"Have Benson check all London flights."

It didn't take long. There weren't that many. Service from Atlanta was new. Art said, "Thanks, Joe, I'll get back to you. I think we'll set up something."

Art put down the receiver and stood up.

"Make us guess," I said.

"Richard Bristow booked himself a Delta nine-oh-five to London. He booked it last night. There wasn't any reservation for Ned Pendergast."

Eric Pender backed out of the doorway. He sat down in the easy chair and closed his eyes. Yes, jobbed and he knew it now.

Eight-forty in the evening.

Art told Hump and me we were out of it. Far out of it. It was Art's show with cooperation from airport security. Implied, but not said, was the thought that he didn't want another screw-up like the one at Peachtree Center.

Hump and I, off to one side, watched him construct the box with both ends closed. A stocky man in a London Fog raincoat, a suitcase at his feet, stood a few feet from the X-ray security machine. He was talking to a woman with orange-red hair. I'd seen Art talking to him. I knew he was the back door.

Art and Joe Benson were the front door. Benson was operating the X-ray machine they ran the carry-on baggage through. Art, with an official clipboard in one hand, looked like clean hands white collar.

"Waiting dries me out," Hump said.

"I think you've got a drinking problem."

"And company," he said.

That was true. I'd have said more but, at that moment, I looked past Hump and saw Ben Pride. He had the stride of a world-beater, a man with some strong commercial purpose in his mind. I knew that walk. The rest of him was different. His hair was black, as it had been in the Houston photo, and he wore a pair of wire-rimmed glasses. His suit was dark brown this time and he carried a leather bag about the size of an attache case but perhaps twice the thickness. Pride reached the feed-in of the X-ray machine and placed the bag, side down, on it.

Art touched the clipboard to his chin. The man in the London Fog hugged the woman with orange-red hair and stepped in behind Ben Pride. Art handed the clipboard to Joe Benson. He crossed to the feed-out section of the X-ray machine. The leather bag bump-bumped out and did a slow turn. Ben Pride reached for the bag. Art stepped in front of him. I saw the glint on the handcuffs, a brief flash, and then Art slapped the cuff on Ben Pride's right wrist. The man in the London Fog moved in fast. He patted Pride down from armpits to ankles.

Ben Pride looked over his shoulder. I think he intended to say something to the man in the London Fog. Instead his eyes fixed on me. That was the first that I realized I was grinning. It was a nasty grin and it nailed Pride. I read it all on his face. Curiosity about me and surprise about what was happening to him. I took that as my cue. I walked over to him. Hump followed a pace behind me. When I was close enough so that I'd be sure he heard me, I said, "Bill Heffner."

"What about him?"

"He scammed you."

I stepped past him. Benson had the leather bag unzipped. Pride had used a section of newspaper to level one end of the stack. The rest of it was cold cash. Bundles and bundles of it. Maybe as much as half a million. Maybe more.

Benson ruffled one bundle. He whistled. Behind me I could hear Art reading Ben Pride his rights from a card.

"It's been satisfactory in every way," Frank Temple said. "I believe I made a wise choice when I hired the two of you."

"It cost a life it didn't have to," I said.

"The con man? What was his name?" He tapped the checks together on the table and jammed them into the envelope.

I didn't answer.

He'd written a check for ten thousand. It was the last payment and it was in front of him on the coffee table. He reached for it. "I'll write another one and add enough to give him a good funeral."

Hump spoke for me. He picked up the check for ten thousand and stuffed it in his pocket. "That's not necessary."

"I'd be glad to." Temple's face had the pseudo-sadness on it, the mark of a funeral director. "It was a bad thing."

"He died with good booze in him," Hump said.

"Well…" Temple felt closed out. He looked about for his top-coat. I'd tossed it on the foot of my bed. "I guess I ought to be going. I might make an early flight back to Boston."

"Good flying," Hump said.

I got his topcoat from the bedroom. On the way past my closet, I reached up and got the .38. I returned to the living room, the gun next to my leg, shielded from him.

Hump helped him with his coat. I switched on the porch light and opened the door. He stepped out first. I followed. His man, Tip, looked up at us, one foot on the bottom step. I'd known he'd be there. Had felt it in my gut.

Temple angled away, avoiding Tip. On the way past he said, "The business is finished, Tip."

"Yes, Mr. Temple." Eyes locked on me.

I brought the .38 away from my side. I tapped it against the front of my right leg. "It worth a kneecap, Tip?"

Tip froze. His hands clenched, turned blue-white.

"Call your dog, Temple."

"Tip."

Tip didn't move at first. His pride was involved and maybe he wanted to believe it was worth a kneecap.

"Tip." There was hard command this time.

Tip backed away. I stood in the doorway while they backed down my drive, until I saw the taillights vanish down the dark road.

Half rain, half sleet fell during the funeral.

Marcy wore her basic black without the pearls and cried a lot. Art stood on that side of the grave with her. He wore the same shiny blue suit he'd been wearing for the last ten years. He looked grim and thoughtful.

Hump and I were on the other side of the grave with the preacher between us. Reverend Houston Mayberry, a Church of

Christer, was the only clergyman we could find to read over Bill. He had bad breath and teeth like blue cheese.

Reverend Mayberry didn't know anything about Bill and he'd assumed he was a businessman. The way he talked about Bill you'd have thought, by dying, Bill had graduated out of the junior Chamber of Commerce here on earth and into that great Chamber of Commerce in the sky.

Some minutes of that and Hump leaned over and told the Reverend to skip all that and go on to the Lord's Prayer.

Mayberry recited it like a little child who didn't understand the words. By rote, without thinking.

I looked up at the sky. Off to the east, above a clump of woods, a single buzzard circled slowly, slowly and then dipped out of sight.

WIND SPIRIT
A SHORT STORY

All things being equal, and this equality being that of disturbed and frightened dreams, it is time to begin. So much garbage in one life and that life only thirty-five years spent. I had not planned to start my autobiography for another twenty-five years. If then. Maybe I'd have waited the full thirty years, for the approaching mellowness, for that one still moment of ripeness before the rot creeps in. No, thunders in, whistles in, explodes upon us. A second consideration: by then, the gall, the bile, might have been thinned down, watered down in the same way that they say the blood of old men is. Waiting, patient, my autobiography might have been charming and whimsical. The reviewers might say: "It brings back an America that doesn't exist anymore." In time, looking back from a distance and blinded by the shapes and shadows of memory, I might have come to believe that my life had its share of charm and beauty. Instead of what it is: a life the parts of which one kicks sand over delicately and moves on, never quite sure later exactly where the lump in the sand really is. Whether I was beaten up by six Japanese policemen in Atsugi or by three bull dykes in San Francisco. Only a few scars over my right eye say that it happened somewhere.

My life to now has been a man's version of what a southern lady's life was once supposed to be. Limited, confined in definition. Born, married, had children, and died.

Born? Check, 1930. In the sandy flat land of South Carolina, in a town called Turbeville. Memories of the violence of both birth and death.

Married? Check, 1960. After the sullen drive down from Chapel Hill until we were across the state line and in South Carolina, in wedlock locked by a J.P. named Angela Slaughter who, in a voice that would have frightened God, asked if we were some of those Chapel Hill reds who believed in integration and that niggers had souls. Before she would sign the marriage certificate we had to assure her that we weren't. Because whatever else we were, finally we were more frightened by the accidental meeting of sperm and egg than we were virtuous about equality.

Had children? Check, one daughter, Evadne. My child in spirit, but never in flesh. The last time I saw Evadne, ugly skinny child with arms and legs knotted like the boles on walking sticks, we were on a beach in Connecticut. Polluted beach. Dead black fish washed up by an oil slick sea. Patterns and swarms of flies. Both walking barefoot on the sand, stepping over the fish. My pale white feet with the sock fuzz still caught under the toenails. Hers bony and tanned, thin and flat as plaster slats. Loving her eye full face, the pale milky blue of marbles. But there was no way of touching her so that she would know and no words that could, with a running start, leap the gap. So that, together, as if by a signal that neither of us had given or had seen, we turned and walked quickly back down the beach to where the car was parked. Disgust and shame, I like to think, in the both of us.

But maybe not in her: perhaps relief instead. Squinting into the overcast sky, still and patient while I brushed the sand from her feet with my handkerchief. Evadne was a polite child to the last. "Come and see me again. Daddy," she said. And I, polite also, said that I would ... soon. A lie between us that calmed the fear we might meet again. That was a year ago, a bit longer, and I have not seen her. Nor does she, I expect, lean on her window sill and wait. Instead, if she leans at her window at all, it is to blow her liquid breath against the cold panes and cloud out any possibility that she will see me.

Divorced? Check, 1964. Not a part of the southern lady's life, but a part of mine. Knowing each other too well, and boredom with what we knew. The chancre in that special rose.

Died? Left blank, not yet. But sometimes I think my whole shabby and discolored life is one prolonged wind sprint toward the grave. (But this is only a heightened sense of melodrama and rhetoric. The other night, parting for the last time from April I said, "All my love before I kick it to death." Knowing quite well that, if one doesn't know what the animal is or where it lives, one has a bit of trouble kicking it to death.) No, I do no wind sprints. My tired body does its own kind of hobbling on. My teeth are bad ... in the last two or three months I've noticed they seem to be loosening, maybe even getting out of line so the uppers and lowers don't match anymore. My hair, almost gone, is grown long on the sides and combed across to cover the bare dome center. The small blood vessels in my face appear to be exploding even as I stand in front of the mirror shaving.

The real problem is genitalia. Oh, not that I've lost the ability to make love. On the contrary. One lady rising shakily from my bed, seen through gritty and swollen eyes of a five o'clock dawn, searching for last night's drink, said, "I thought all the great lovers had left town."

I, for want of a better thing to say, answered, "I just got back to town."

"Stay awhile then," she said, "and welcome back."

AndI, polite again, said, "Thank you," while another part of me said, "Go home."

Two nights ago, at April's apartment, angry at her because she suddenly moved toward the edge of the bed and said that she was hungry ... out of anger I made love to her like I think rape must be.

Violating my whole sense of myself and my sense of her. In the breath guttering, the afterwards, I found that I was crying out of this same anger, out of frustration, out of shame that I had found the rapist inside me. I had to hide it, pushing my face into the pillow and blotting against the pillow case... but perhaps a drop fell on her shoulder. At least, she noticed.

"1 know why you're crying."

I asked why.

"Because it was so beautiful."

Which made me wonder.

I don't know what has happened. Something has. Maybe as recently as the last two or three months. A loss of soul, a death of the spirit.

Or, because words mean nothing, a loss of spirit, a death of then-soul. High and serious terms for this special malaise. I have trouble with words now. I am not a professional writer. I am beyond all hope of that now. In fact, the whole effort to mend my bridges, to protect myself in case the writing came to nothing, has provided me with a good job here at the University. Teaching theater history. "Describe Hanswurst's costume in detail. What were Goethe's rules for action? W.B. Yeat's attitude toward Ibsen and what does it mean?"

The dissertation started and put aside has yet to be done. The students with their basic understanding of what flattery really is call me Doctor. I do not correct them because it takes time away from the class when other more important matters have to be treated, and, I sometimes think, it would be unkind to embarrass them. The notes on the sociological aspects of medieval French drama fade in my carefully kept and carefully avoided filing cabinet. Until the sap and energy rise again.

April. Nymph. Between eighteen and nineteen years old. Strange to picture myself beside her pale blonde image. Last Saturday, at the football game with her, pushing past knees toward our seats, I heard one of the co-eds we passed say, "He must be her father." I looked at April to see if she'd heard and found that she was blushing.

I guess I am her father, both of us loving the scent of ritual incest.

The green rank scent of it. Acting out in gesture and a language neither of us understands the closet drama in which the surface is more important than the depths. Once, trying to explain this to her, I said that I was writing my own Poetics. "The modem tragic hero is a man committed to something which he knows in his own heart to be absurd."

"What is absurd?" she asked. Incest and oatmeal cookies.

After a moment: "You haven't answered me." I know. "I guess you're not going to answer me."

Pouting. A muscle coils in her back. Ending in the rigid little toe of her left foot. On the side of which there is the centerless pit of a corn.

Words bubble, child, but there is no answer.

"Sometimes I don't think you appreciate my intelligence."

"It is your mind I love most," I say.

The muscle uncoils and the com disappears under the twisted edge of the sheet.

"Daddy you been on my mind," April whispers. A smile which I answer. Then, dully, outside my window, the sharp crack of acorns falling upon unraked leaves. The crack of ice or sleet.

"Child ..." I say, now that she is under my wing, her nose wrinkling against the gracing hair of my chest ... "Child, winter is not only coming. It is here."

April blows rings of hot wet air against my chest. "It'll be alright. Daddy." And between the even, smooth, matching teeth she clamps one of the gray hairs and jerking back her head tears it out.

The next morning, an hour before my first class, as I stepped into the shower I noticed the pitpoint cake of blood where the hair had been. During the shower the cake dissolved, revealing the pit open and dark, without a bottom.

Afternoon now. Winter light afternoon. Somewhere, somewhere between Harry's and The Tempo, with a gray hair clutched between her teeth like a flower, April has decided to find herself a young man. Daddies are all-right, but young men reflect like windows and brightly polished sports cars. Done, enough.

And let him kick it to death if he can find it.

Winter light afternoon. The slow rain has not stopped, but has frozen into a wall. From my window, from my office high above, I watch students walk through the wall. It seems much easier than it probably is.

This short story was originally published in the Spring 1967 issue of the literary magazine *Lillabulero: Being a Periodical of Literature and the Arts*, which was edited by Russell Banks.

ABOUT THE AUTHOR

Ralph Dennis isn't a household name...but he should be. He is widely considered among crime writers as a master of the genre, denied the recognition he deserved because his twelve *Hardman* books, which are beloved and highly sought-after collectables now, were poorly packaged in the 1970s by Popular Library as a cheap men's action-adventure paperbacks with numbered titles.

Even so, some top critics saw past the cheesy covers and noticed that he was producing work as good as John D. MacDonald, Raymond Chandler, Chester Himes, Dashiell Hammett, and Ross MacDonald.

The *New York Times* praised the *Hardman* novels for "expert writing, plotting, and an unusual degree of sensitivity. Dennis has mastered the genre and supplied top entertainment." The *Philadelphia Daily News* proclaimed *Hardman* "the best series around, but they've got such terrible covers..."

Unfortunately, Popular Library didn't take the hint and continued to present the series like hack work, dooming the novels to a short shelf-life and obscurity...except among generations of crime writers, like novelist Joe R. Lansdale (the *Hap & Leonard* series) and screenwriter Shane Black (the *Lethal Weapon* movies), who've kept Dennis' legacy alive through word-of-mouth and by acknowledging his influence on their stellar work.

Ralph Dennis wrote three other novels that were published outside of the *Hardman* series but he wasn't able to reach the wide audience, or gain the critical acclaim, that he deserved during his lifetime.

He was born in 1931 in Sumter, South Carolina, and received a masters degree from University of North Carolina, where he later taught film and television writing after serving a stint in the Navy. At the time of his death in 1988, he was working at a bookstore in Atlanta and had a file cabinet full of unpublished novels.

Brash Books will be releasing the entire *Hardman* series, his three other published novels, and his long-lost manuscripts.